Dope Girl Magic

Lock Down Publications and Ca$h Presents Dope Girl Magic A Novel by *Destiny Skai*

Dope Girl Magic

Lock Down Publications
P.O. Box 870494
Mesquite, Tx 75187

Visit our site at
www.lockdownpublications.com

Copyright 2020 by Destiny Skai
Dope Girl Magic

Lock Down Publications
Like our page on Facebook: Lock Down Publications
@
www.facebook.com/lockdownpublications.ldp
Cover design and layout by: **Dynasty Cover Me**
Book interior design by: **Shawn Walker**
Edited by: **Kiera Northington**

3

Stay Connected with Us!

Text **LOCKDOWN** to 22828 to stay up-to-date with new releases, sneak peaks, contests and more…

Thank you!

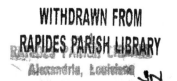

Submission Guideline.

Submit the first three chapters of your completed manuscript to ldpsubmissions@gmail.com, subject line: Your book's title. The manuscript must be in a .doc file and sent as an attachment. Document should be in Times New Roman, double spaced and in size 12 font. Also, provide your synopsis and full contact information. If sending multiple submissions, they must each be in a separate email.

Have a story but no way to send it electronically? You can still submit to LDP/Ca$h Presents. Send in the first three chapters, written or typed, of your completed manuscript to:

LDP: Submissions Dept
Po Box 870494
Mesquite, Tx 75187

DO NOT send original manuscript. Must be a duplicate.

Provide your synopsis and a cover letter containing your full contact information.

Thanks for considering LDP and Ca$h Presents.

Prologue
March 5, 2008

"Happy birthday to you, happy birthday to you. Happy birthday, dear Tori. Happy birthday to you." Tori leaned closer to her four-tier cake, closed her eyes and blew out the two candles that represented her sixteenth birthday, a number one and a six.

"Yayyy!" the crowd shouted and cheered after she made her wish.

Tears of joy surfaced in the wells of her eyes, but she quickly wiped them away. "Thanks, everyone. Y'all know how to make a girl feel special."

Happily standing to the left, stood her parents, Diesel and Bianca, to ensure their one and only child had a night she would never forget. "I pray all your dreams come true, princess." Diesel kissed her forehead. "I love you. Enjoy the party. I'll be back in the morning."

"I love you too, Daddy."

Bianca also kissed her and repeated the same exact words to her baby girl. "I love you too, Mommy."

Bianca was a beautiful, dark chocolate bombshell. Her makeup was flawless. It covered the dark rings underneath her eyes and the track marks embedded on her skin. Diesel was the biggest dope dealer hailing out of West Palm Beach, Florida, and his wife was a certified junkie. He fed her and the streets grade-A dope.

Bianca wasn't your average junkie. She graduated at the top of her class with a dream to pursue a career as a pharmacist. But one fateful night changed all of that.

One late night when her shift was over, Bianca walked out into the parking lot, where she was robbed at gunpoint and shot in the stomach. At the time, she was eight months pregnant with their first son, Torin Price Jr. A passerby found her on the ground and immediately called the police. Sadly, the baby didn't make it and her world was flipped upside down.

Unable to bounce back from the pain stabbing at her heart and eating at her flesh, Bianca quit her job and abandoned her family. Diesel issued a bounty for her safe return. A week later, when he finally found her, she was strung out on dope and sleeping inside a crack house. Immediately, she was put into rehab for six months before she was released. Things had begun to look up for the family, until the one-year anniversary of the shooting crept around. Bianca relapsed and started back using. From that day to the present, she hadn't stopped using and Diesel was tired of trying to force her to be clean. Ultimately, he gave up. The battle was no longer his and he could no longer force it, if that was the life she chose.

"I see how that boy keeps looking at you." Bianca smiled as she pushed hair from her daughter's face.

Tori giggled like a bashful child. "What boy?"

"Kilo. You can hide it from your father, but not from me. I was a teenage girl before, baby."

Tori looked away once her cover was blown. "Please don't tell Dad."

"Never, baby. Your secret is safe with me. Just be safe and discreet. If he finds out it won't end well, I promise."

Confusion was embedded on her pretty face. "What do you mean?"

"Don't worry about your father. Men never likes who their daughters date, especially when they don't like the father of the boy she's dating. I'll handle him. Live your life with no regrets and be happy."

"Thanks, Mom." Tori hugged her queen once more, then pushed her questions to the back of her skull. Their conversation was far from over. She needed to know what happened between Diesel and Eazy.

Kilo waited until the coast was clear to approach Tori. "Happy birthday, baby." He pulled out a small gold box with a white ribbon. "I love you."

Her eyes shined bright like diamonds as she opened her gift. Inside was a gold Rolex watch with diamonds. "I love you too, baby, and my gift."

Kilo grinned and shook his head. "But you didn't look at the details of it. Take it out the box and tell me what you see."

Tori removed the expensive timepiece. The face of the watch had a selfie of the couple kissing. "Baeee! I love it," she screeched.

"Flip it over." The back of the watch read, *Kilo and Tori. Always and forever.*

Tori hugged his neck tight for a brief amount of time, before she let go. "What made you get me this? I really love it."

"When it comes to me and you, I need you to know what time it is. Fuck who don't like it, including your daddy."

"Baeeee! You so corny, but I love you so much. And don't worry about that. My mama knows and she's all for it."

"At least somebody cool with it besides my dad."

"He'll come around," Tori assured him. "If not, I'll be eighteen in two years."

"I'll wait forever if that means we can finally be together in peace."

"That's why I love you." Tori looked around to make sure no one was watching before she kissed his lips.

One hour later, the party was still jumping and damn near everybody was tipsy as hell. Tori and Kilo were dancing and enjoying themselves without a care in the world. Tori had a buzz from the hunch punch Bianca slipped her and some of her friends. It had her slightly aggressive and horny. "Come on. Let's sneak away."

"And go where?" Kilo asked out of curiosity.

"To my room."

"Hell nah! You trying to get me killed."

"No, I'm not. My dad left for business and my mama don't care. She probably in her own world right now," she stated, referring to Bianca being someplace high out her mind. "Let's go before someone notices we're gone."

"I didn't bring no condoms."

"Just don't cum in me. Simple." Kilo was high and tipsy, so he agreed. Tori grabbed his hand and left the backyard.

Just as suspected, Bianca was higher than a kite. The couple crept up to her room unnoticed and closed the door behind them. Once the locks were secured, they both got naked and rushed towards the bed. Two weeks prior, Kilo had taken Tori's virginity and she'd been hooked on the dick the same way her mama was hooked on dope. So, instead of fear, anxiousness caressed her horny flesh.

Tori laid on her back and opened wide for her man. Kilo slid his body over hers and entered her slowly. Her body raised just a bit, as she placed her warm hands on his strong back. Kilo thrusted in and out with complete tenderness. Every opportunity he received to make passionate love to her was better than the last. Their lips found each other through the lustful moans, allowing their tongues to connect.

The feeling of Kilo surfing her walls was a pleasure she had never felt before. A feeling she refused to lose. Even if it caused problems in her household, she was never going to leave Kilo alone. The love they shared was like Romeo and Juliet. The thought alone caused a single tear to fall from her eye, as she stared passionately into his dark, scary eyes.

"Why you crying?" Seeing her cry made him pause mid-stroke.

"I just love you so much."

"I love you too, bae." Now that he knew she was fine, Kilo pushed her knees up to her chest and got back to work. His eyes were glued on her middle, as he watched his piece glide in and out of her sweet nookie. Her pussy had his dick in the chokehold, forcing his nut to surface. Instead of allowing it to release, he pulled out and smacked his hand against her thigh.

"It's time to ride."

"But bae, I don't know how to," Tori pouted.

Kilo pecked her on the lips. "Practice makes perfect. Now get up and do what I taught you."

Tori straddled his lap, took a deep breath and eased down slowly on his wood. Kilo grunted from the satisfaction and held her hips. The movement of her hips started out slow. Two minutes later, she rode it with ease with assistance from her tutor.

"Fuck, bae! Ride that dick just like that."

"Ahh! Ahh! Ouuu…shit," she moaned.

One thing Tori knew was how an orgasm felt. Kilo made sure she had that experience. Although he was only eighteen, that young nigga knew how to slang that dingaling. Which was why he had Tori's mind so gone.

While grinning at the funny faces she made, Kilo used his thumb to stroke her love button. His touch was tender. The feeling was euphoric and she could no longer contain herself. Kilo could feel her walls pulsating against his shaft right before he felt a gush of fluid saturate his flesh.

"Keep going. Mine coming," he mumbled. Tori gave into his request until she felt him squeeze her hips and bite down on his lip. "Damn, bae. Shit!"

Whenever Kilo did that, she knew he was busting. Immediately, she remembered he wasn't wearing any protection. "Bae, don't nut in me, please," she moaned.

Kilo was barely listening, being that he was trying to concentrate on getting off. Without a warning, he erupted heavily, while grunting heavily. His grip loosened.

Tori hopped off the dick. "Bae, what I told you?"

"Shit. My bad, bae. I tried to pull out, but I couldn't."

"I bet."

"You nutted on me, so I can nut in you," he chuckled.

"You better hope nothing happened."

"Girl, you not gone get pregnant. Chill out."

"I better not." Tori pouted as she snuggled underneath her soldier.

"We good," he promised.

Kilo kissed her forehead and closed his eyes. The effects of the intoxicants had them both in a slumber. Light snoring could be heard throughout the room, along with the sound of the central AC unit that chilled the atmosphere.

Boom! Boom!

The sound of the door crashing to the floor startled the sleeping couple. Tori and Kilo jumped up, with the blanket covering their nude bodies, only to find Diesel moving swiftly in their direction.

"Daddy!" Tori screeched.

"What the fuck this nigga doing in my house? And in your bed for that matter? You fuckin' now?" he screamed.

Diesel reached out to snatch Kilo up, but he was quickly apprehended by his right-hand man Byrd. "Yo, D, calm down."

"Nigga, don't tell me to calm the fuck down when my daughter in here taking dick from Eazy son."

"All I'm saying is think before you react. This could turn out bad and start an unnecessary war between camps."

Diesel gritted his teeth and glared into his partner's eyes. "You think I give a fuck about a war?"

While he wasn't paying attention, Tori and Kilo slipped on their clothes. There was no telling what Diesel might do, but he had to keep his cool. There was no way he could show weakness. Especially not in front of his girl. Fear wasn't a trait his father cursed him with. Diesel thought for a second before turning back towards the frightened teens.

"Tori, you are on punishment until the day you leave for college. As for you," he shot daggers in Kilo's direction, "this is my last time saying this. Don't ever step foot on my property and don't let me catch you within a thousand feet of my daughter. Consider this promise your restraining order."

The loud voices and screaming sent Bianca into the room. Her cloudy, red eyes landed on her baby girl. The tears that stained Tori's face sent her in a rage. Bianca ran up on Diesel and slapped him twice.

Whap! Whap!

The last slap had him heated. Diesel grabbed her wrists and squeezed tightly. "You get two of those. Next time, you gone get what you deserve."

Bianca freed herself from his grip. "Get the fuck off me before you get more than you bargaining for."

Diesel's eyes formed into tiny, dark slits. Ones that resembled a snake. "You heard what the fuck I said. Now take your ass back to your room, before you end up in the emergency room."

Bianca's stare was cold as ice. "Fuck you and your worthless ass threats. I care about that just as much as I care about your black, arrogant ass." She put her finger in his face. "Leave my child alone before I bury yo' ass next to that bitch you called mama."

Before she could blink, Diesel backhanded her, sending her crashing to the floor. "Daddy, stop!" Tori screamed. Kilo used the distraction as a chance for him to break out like a bandit without anyone noticing except Tori.

Diesel stood over Bianca. "You better be lucky I have respect the size of a mustard seed, 'cause I'll knock yo' junky ass into a coma."

"Stop it!" Tori screamed.

"Fuck you!" she spat. "It's your fault I'm hooked on this shit in the first place."

Diesel immediately felt bad and regretted the words that left his mouth. He knew she was high. That was the only time she spoke on his dead mother. In an effort to calm the atmosphere, he reached down and pulled Bianca to her feet. "I'm sorry."

"You meant what you said." Bianca left the room without another word.

"Whatever, man. I'll deal with you later." Diesel turned back to Tori. "Where did that nigga go?"

"He left, D." Byrd nodded towards the door.

"And that's the type of nigga you wanna fuck? That nigga didn't bother to stick around and face me like a man." Diesel stepped in closer to shorten their distance. "Don't let me catch you with him again and I'm dead ass serious."

"You can't do that. We don't have anything to do with whatever beef you have with Eazy. We're in love."

Diesel chuckled. "Love. You think that nigga love you? Come on now, I raised you better than that. You see he ran his bitch ass out of here."

"Stick around for what? To battle with you and lose. I wish I could've left with him."

"Yo ass ain't leaving this muthafuckin' room. So, you might as well get comfortable. I'm buying you a chastity belt. Let's go, Byrd." Tori flopped down on the bed once Diesel and his henchman left the room. The ache in her heart made her an emotional mess. Tears streamed down her face as she laid down and cuddled her pillow. Kilo's scent lingered on the fabric. As she closed her eyes and cried, Tori eventually fell asleep with Kilo on her mind.

***

"What the fuck is wrong with you? Did you know she was fucking that nigga?" Diesel paced the floor while shouting at Bianca.

"Yeah. I did know that. What's the problem?"

"She's sixteen and has no business having sex."

Bianca giggled and flicked the ashes from her cigarette into the ashtray. "Did you forget what we were doing at that age?"

"I don't give a fuck about what we did. This is my daughter we're talking about. That shit ain't cool, Bianca."

"No shit, stupid. That's my daughter too. You can't stop her from having sex. Neither can I so get over it. Just be glad she not out here fucking any and everybody. Kilo is her boyfriend."

Bianca sat the cigarette down and opened the dresser drawer. Inside was an eight-ball of pure, uncut powder. That instantly set him off. Diesel snatched the clear plastic bag that housed the product.

"This why you don't give a fuck about nothing. You too busy getting high to realize what Tori is doing is wrong."

Bianca stood up and attempted to take her happy medicine back. "Give me my shit. I don't wanna talk to you."

"You don't have a fuckin' choice. Now sit the fuck down before I knock you down."

Bianca backed up and opened the drawer once more. This time she pulled out a small handgun and aimed it at her husband. "If you put your hands on me again, nigga, I will kill your motherfucking ass. Now play with me."

Diesel remained calm. A huge part of him knew she wouldn't pull the trigger, but a tiny part of him said not to push her. Bianca was high and he didn't want to underestimate her. "You're not going to shoot me, so put that up before you hurt yourself."

"The only person I want to hurt is you."

"Why? Because I don't agree that Tori should be having sex or messing with Kilo?"

"You and I both know we can't stop her from seeing him." Bianca waved the gun in the air. "This isn't about Kilo. It's about Eazy and the hatred you have towards him. From what I can see, Kilo loves Tori and you need to accept that fact."

"Fuck Eazy. It's your fault all of this went down in the first place."

"Yeah, blame me, since that's easier than accepting your role in all of this. At one point in time the two of you were inseparable. You allowed pussy to get in the way of that. No one is to blame except you. All this shit is your fucking fault, Diesel, so get over it!" Bianca screamed with tears in her eyes.

"I didn't make you fuck that nigga."

"Well, if you hadn't fucked his girl, I wouldn't have fucked your brother. That's called karma."

"That ain't my brother."

"Well, step-brother, if that makes you feel better. At the end of the day, you are the one to blame." Bianca wiped her eyes. "Do you know why I despise you so much? I lost my son because of you." Her voice elevated. "I hate you. I fucking hate you. I can't stand seeing your face. You didn't protect me. You wasn't there when I needed you that night, because you was laid up with that bitch Chasity. Now give me my shit so I can get high and forget about the misery I'm living in being here with you."

Those words hit Diesel in the chest. It made him weak because a lot of what she spoke on was the truth. "Damn, you don't love me anymore?"

"No. I haven't loved you since the day I lost my son." Her response was harsh and nonchalant.

Afraid of the answer that was to follow his next question, he took a deep breath, preparing for the painful truth. "You keep saying your son. Was that even my son?"

"No. He wasn't your son."

Diesel's heart stopped beating for a split second. Deep down inside, that was always a question he had pushed to the back of his mind. But he was too afraid to ask back then. Diesel wanted to hurt her badly, but it wasn't worth it. Bianca wasn't worth seeing him shed a single tear. She made it clear that she no longer loved him. The sad and crazy thing was he still loved her, despite her indiscretions. Diesel left the room for a good ten minutes to get his thoughts together. When he came back, he was fuming and Bianca was still complaining about getting high.

"You said a lot of hurtful shit just now, but I'm going to give you a pass. I've done a lot of shit I'm not proud of, but at the end of the day, I never intentionally hurt you the way you did me."

Diesel tossed the powder on the bed. "Smoke your life away. Destroy yourself. You love this more than me anyway."

"You goddamn right. The drugs never lied to me."

Diesel didn't reply. He just walked away and went into his bedroom.

***

Tori was awakened by loud shouting. Certain that her parents were probably fighting, she jumped up and rushed towards the commotion. As she ran down the hallway, she realized the noise was coming from her mother's bedroom. Diesel and Byrd were kneeling down beside Bianca, who was sprawled out on the floor. Quickly, she rushed towards them and the sight of white foam coming from her mother's mouth caused her to scream.

"Mommy!"

Diesel looked up. "Tori, go downstairs and wait on the ambulance."

"No! What's wrong with her?"

"She's overdosing. We're waiting on help to come."

Bianca was shaking uncontrollably. Tori dropped to her knees and grabbed her arm. "Mommy! Mommy! Get up. Please." She screamed and cried.

One hour later

Diesel sat in the waiting room of the hospital, waiting on the doctor to come back with an update on Bianca's condition. He held Tori tight in his arms as she cried.

"I'm sorry you had to witness that, baby. Your mom is sick."

"Why won't you help her?"

"I tried, baby. Believe me I did. Bianca doesn't want help. This is what she wants to do."

Tori sat up and wiped her face with her sweater. "Daddy, promise you'll help Mom. I just want us to be a family again."

Diesel closed his eyes and took a deep breath. When he opened them, Tori was staring in his eyes. "I'll put her back in rehab, but we won't be a family again. Your mother doesn't love me anymore. She told me that tonight."

"Mom does love you. She told me."

Before he could respond, the doctor approached him. "Mr. Price?"

"Yes."

"My staff and I did everything we could do to save your wife, but nothing helped. I'm sorry to say this, but she's gone. I'm sorry for your loss."

Tori jumped from her seat and rushed towards the same door the doctor emerged from. "Mommy. Nooooo!" Diesel ran behind her to console his grieving child on her birthday.

Chapter 1
Three years later

The all-white Lexus IS250 pulled up in front of the store and came to a screeching halt. Two dudes engaged in a conversation, standing on the corner, turned to face the noise.

"Do you need me to get out with you?" Kilo asked, while clutching his pistol.

"Nah, I got it. You'll know if I need reinforcement." Tori stepped from the car dressed in a pair of tight fitted jeans, a crop top sweater and a pair of Christian Louboutin thigh-high boots. The twenty-two-inch sew in weave she wore hung past the middle of her back. In her hand, she clutched a chrome 9-millimeter handgun.

Swiftly, she approached one of her workers. "What's good, Boss Lady?" Jarvis asked nervously.

"You tell me, Jarvis. What the fuck did we discuss the last time I saw you?"

"Umm. That." He was so scared, he couldn't get his words right. "You said to make sure I had your money on time."

"Exactly and that's why I'm having a hard time trying to figure out why in the fuck would you go behind my back and talk to my father. You work for me, not him."

"I know. I'm sorry. I just wanted to try and buy some more time. Shit been rough for me, but I swear I'm going to get the money up. Just give me a few more days and—" Before he could get another word in Tori brought the cold piece of steel across his skull.

Jarvis grabbed his head with his left hand. Blood oozed from the wound. Embarrassment was all he felt at that moment, but he knew he couldn't retaliate out of fear of Diesel and Kilo. The guy he was talking to backed up a few feet. He knew all about Tori and knew she wasn't to be played with.

"Next time I tell your bitch ass something, you don't run back to my father. He can't tell me shit. You got that?"

"Yes."

"Yes, what?" She placed her hand on her hip.

"Yes, Boss Lady. I got it."

"Good. You have forty-eight hours to run me my money or next time, you gone get a bullet to your skull. Consider this your warning."

Tori strutted back to the car and climbed inside. Kilo smiled and licked his lips. "Damn, you just looked sexy as hell doing that shit."

"Oh really?"

"Fuck yeah. You made my dick hard." When he left the streets eighteen months ago, his lady wasn't ruthless. However, he was happy with what he came home to.

Tori looked down at his print before leaning in and kissing his lips. "I think I can help you with that."

"I know you can. Let's go to the house then, shit."

"Nah. Let's get a room. We'll give your dad some privacy tonight." Tori smirked and pulled off. "I'm sure he tired of sneaking that lady over there like we wouldn't notice."

Kilo chuckled. "Yeah, that nigga think he slick."

"Besides, I want to try out this pole I bought."

"Oh, hell yeah." Kilo pulled out his cell.

"What you doing?"

"I'm about to book us a penthouse suite for the weekend. Drop me off to the house so I can pack a bag."

"I don't have to drop you off."

"Yeah, you do. You need to go home and pack too."

"My bag is packed and in the trunk already."

"Oh, you had this planned out already."

"Yep." Tori flushed it to Kilo's crib. She was ready to lay up with her dude for the next three days with no interruptions. It was about to be nothing but sex, alcohol and no phones.

Thirty minutes later they were pulling up to Kilo's mini mansion, where he lived with his father, Eazy. Before Tori could kill the engine, her phone rang. Kilo looked down at the screen and shook his head when he saw Dazzle's name pop up.

"There goes your patient."

"Why do you always say that?" She grabbed the phone. "All she want is some advice for that dysfunctional ass relationship she in. That bitch need to start paying you for wasting your time, 'cause she ain't gone leave him."

"You know I don't encourage my friends to leave their niggas. Those are grown ass women and they gone do what they see fit."

"The power of dick. I'll never understand it." Kilo opened the door and got out. "I'll be upstairs when you ready."

"This won't take long, baby."

"Okay."

Tori answered the phone once Kilo closed the door. "Hey, girl. What's going on?"

Dazzle sighed. "Girl, everything. I'm sick of this nigga. I swear, he's getting on my last motherfucking nerve."

"Oh Lord, what done happened now?" Tori sat back and got comfortable. She knew this conversation was about to be long and pointless.

"The same old shit. This nigga always has something to say about my fucking job. I'm getting tired of explaining the same shit over and over again."

"I don't understand what the problem is. He met you in the strip club. Ain't shit changed except y'all had a baby and that's it. He knew that was how you made your money."

Dazzle was sniffling. She had been crying for the longest time and ready to explode. "He keep bringing up the fact that his homeboys can see me naked at any time."

"Oh well, they shouldn't be in there looking. Tell Tron's ass if he wants you out the club, then he needs to step up and take care of the household."

"He can't cause he's too busy playing fucking videos and smoking weed all day. This nigga think he's a house dad or some shit. I'm sick of him."

"No, you not. You just mad at the moment."

"I am."

"I'll never tell you to just up and leave him. I'm not that type of friend, but once you get really tired, you'll send him back to his mama house."

"Yeah you right. But, why is it an issue? I been doing this shit way before him."

"And you gone stop doing that shit too. You always telling them hoes our motherfucking business." Tron shouted in the background.

Tori bit her bottom lip out of frustration. "I'm not gone respond to that bitch, because I'll tell him about his bald-headed ass mammy."

"Girl, he stupid. Ignore him," Dazzle added.

"Bitch, you stupid. You better watch your motherfucking mouth before I pop you in it." Tron tried to snatch her phone.

"Shut the fuck up!" Dazzle shouted.

"Girl, just call me later."

"I will."

Tori ended the call and got out the car. Upon entering the home, she walked in and stood face-to-face with Eazy. "Hey pops. How you doing?"

"I'm good, baby girl. How you doing?"

"I'm good." Tori smiled, as she watched Kilo ascend down the steps.

"Where y'all headed?" Eazy looked at the duffle bag Kilo was toting.

"Away for the weekend," Kilo replied.

"We know you want some privacy," Tori added.

"Be safe. I know how Diesel feel about y'all being together and I don't want no problems out of him. You just got out of prison and I don't need you going back."

"We good, Pops. Don't worry," Kilo assured him before dapping him up and walking out the door.

***

Dazzle was trying her best to ignore Tron so she could get ready for her shift at the strip club, but he wasn't letting up at all. He kept following her around the apartment, talking shit.

"That's what we do now? Disrespect me in front of your homegirl? Do you think Tori would ever disrespect Kilo like that? Fuck no! She knows how to treat and respect her nigga. She on her grown woman shit. Something you need to be studying."

Dazzle rolled her eyes and flicked him off. "Don't speak on my sister. She don't fuck with you at all."

"You think I give a fuck about that? I'm just stating facts." Tron grabbed his blunt from the ashtray and lit it. "I know one fuckin' thing. You better start respecting me as your man and listening to what I tell you."

"I'm not listening to shit." Dazzle faced Tron with a mean mug. "Until you start bringing some real money up in this bitch, I'm not listening to shit you say. A boy can't tell me shit. Holla at me when you become a real man like Kilo. Then maybe I'll listen like Tori."

Steam came from Tron's ears, as he listened to the disrespectful comments flying from his babymama's tongue. Tron sat the blunt down and stood up. Dazzle had a look of uncertainty on her face. Once he was close enough to grab her, he wrapped his hand around the base of her throat.

"You better watch the way you talk to me." His grip tightened when he had her back against the wall. Dazzle tried to loosen his grip and catch her breath, but he squeezed tighter. That was when she decided to fight back. Dazzle used her knee to hit him in the balls. Tron immediately released his grip. "Bitch," he yelled, while backhanding her in the face.

Whap!

Tron didn't expect Dazzle to do anything until he felt her fist connect with his jaw. It was that moment all hell broke loose. Tron and Dazzle were in the living room, going blow for blow like two bitches in the streets. The fight lasted all of two minutes, but to Dazzle it felt like an eternity. Their son, Jamir, walked into the living room holding his sippy cup and crying. Tron immediately stopped hitting Dazzle and focused on his child.

"Hey fat daddy. We woke you up." He leaned down and picked up his son. Then he looked back at Dazzle. "I meant what I said."

"And so did I," she snapped. "I'm going to work and that's the end of discussion."

"Do it and watch I make you regret that shit."

"Whatever, Tron." She laughed and walked off.

"The same thing that makes you laugh, will make you cry." He grabbed Jamir's empty cup and went into the kitchen.

Dazzle grabbed her things to shower with and headed to the bathroom. Upon entering, she stopped in front of the mirror and checked her appearance. There was a slight bruise underneath her right eye and her bottom lip was split.

"Nothing a little make-up can't fix." Forty-five minutes later, she was fully dressed and ready to go to work. On her way out, she gave Jamir a kiss.

"So, you still going to work, huh?"

"Yep. So, don't wait up."

Dazzle smirked and walked out the door just as Tron shouted, "You gone regret this."

Tron's blood was bubbling under his flesh like boiling grits. After putting Jamir back to sleep, he sat on the porch to catch some fresh air. He pulled out a grape Swisher Sweet and twisted up a fat blunt. Rolled tight and in between his fingertips, Tron put it to his lips and took a heavy pull. The weed was so potent, he immediately felt a rush. Heavy coughing followed soon after.

"This that gas," he stated while taking another pull.

Loud talking and giggles could be heard from a short distance. When he looked up, he saw Mya coming down the sidewalk in a short skirt and a halter top. "Hey, Tron," she giggled.

Tron pushed his dreads from out of his face. "Sup git."

"Bitch, I'm a call you back." Mya ended the call and stopped directly in front of her crush. "Boy, stop calling me git. I'm grown."

"Girl, please. Yo' ass hardly grown if you still in high school."

Mya sucked her teeth. "Boy, bye. What the fuck that got to do with anything?"

"It means you a little ass girl and I only fuck with grown ass bitches."

"Age ain't nothing but a number. Besides, this pussy grown." Mya placed her hand between her legs, then slowly raised her skirt, showing her bald kitty.

Tron laughed in her face. "That's a baby pussy. I bet that lil' shit pissy 'cause you still wiping back to front."

Mya was highly irritated with his sarcasm. She couldn't believe he was hurling insults her way, but he wasn't about to get away with trying her. To shut him up, she grabbed his hand and placed it directly between her lips. "I bet this pussy have your grown ass hooked."

Tron didn't move his hand. In fact, he was curious if she knew how to fuck. It ate his soul, so he brought his hand up to his nose for a smell test. "Okay, I was wrong. She don't smell pissy."

"Bitch, I know how to clean my shit. Stop playing with me." Tron pinched her lip hard. "Stop playing with me and watch your tongue, lil' ass girl."

"Ouch!" She jumped. "Tron, stop. That shit hurt."

"That's exactly what I'd have you saying if I fucked your young ass. You can't handle grown dick." Tron freed her lip. "Take yo' ass in the house before you get in trouble."

"Nah, I'm trying to go in the house with you."

"Girl, you don't want this. I'll have yo' ass climbing the walls."

"I do have cat in my blood, so what's up? I know you wanna fuck me. I be seeing how you be looking at me." Mya scanned the parking lot for Dazzle's car. "Where's your babymama? At work?"

"Yeah." Tron stroked his chin and thought back to the way Dazzle disrespected him earlier. "Fuck her. Come inside the crib. She won't be back until early morning."

Mya licked her lips. "I knew you would change your mind."

"You better be able to handle this log, 'cause I'ma beat your back out." Mya stepped inside behind Tron and closed the door. She had been waiting and plotting for the chance to snatch up

Dazzle's baby daddy, so quite naturally, she didn't care about fucking him in their bed. That had been a dream of hers since the day she met him.

Chapter 2

Kilo and Tori pulled up in front of the club in his brandy wine convertible. The valet attendant walked up to the car as Kilo stepped out, dripping in expensive threads and jewelry.

"You scratch it, you bought it." The young fella smiled, as they dapped each other up.

"Come on, Kilo. You know I got you, bro."

"You better." Kilo walked to the passenger seat and opened the door for his queen.

Grabbing her hand, he escorted her from the car and they approached the building. Kilo was well known and respected in every hood, so they let the couple in with no problem. Inside, the music was bumping and the strippers were getting their money. Tori's eyes landed on the stage and she recognized her girl, Dazzle, gliding down the pole.

They maneuvered to the VIP section where Kilo's homeboys, Fresh and Milo were chilling. Tori spoke, then sat down and opened her phone to send a quick text in a group message with Dazzle, Lala and Tweety to let them know where they could find her.

Kilo stood, chopping it up with his boys over the music, with the bottle of Patrón clutched in his hand. Fixing a cup, he handed to Tori.

"Thanks, baby." Tori took a sip and checked out the crowd. She was in her own little world bumping to the music.

Tori's eyes never left Kilo. She could stare at him for hours without batting a lash. When Kilo was arrested and sentenced to fourteen months, Tori thought she would die without her other half. However, she kept in touch with him during his entire bid. It wasn't an easy task, being that she could not receive his letters at home, so Eazy passed them along with no problem.

For the past four months, they were able to keep their relationship low-key. That was the only way to maintain the peace in their lives and to keep Diesel out of their business. Kilo glanced into Tori's eyes and smiled. The chemistry they shared was hotter than fish grease. He leaned down and whispered in her ear, "Why you keep looking at me like that?"

Tori ran her tongue across his lips. "Cause you looking real edible right now."

"You so nasty," he grinned.

"Only for you."

"Better be."

"You know I love only you."

"I love you too. And when we leave here, I'll show you just how much I do." Kilo kissed her soft lips, ignoring the shiny lip gloss that coated them. "Where your homegirls at?"

"I don't know. I texted them." Tori then looked down at her phone, only to realize that she had a missed call and text from Lala. "Oh, Lala just said they're outside."

"Good. I know you want to vibe with your girls."

Tori stood up and wrapped her arms around his waist. "Of course, but not more than I want to vibe with you."

Just as Kilo was about to respond, he was cut off. "You too fine to be hugging this lame ass nigga."

Kilo stood erect to get a good look at who he needed to knock out. The dude stood there grinning. All Kilo could do was shake his head. "Nigga, you was about to get fucked up on the house."

"Bro, you should've seen your face." Honcho hugged his big brother. Then he hugged Tori. "What's up, sis?"

"Nothing much." She took a step back to get a good look at him. "Damn, Honcho, I haven't seen you since you left for college. What the hell you been eating? You big as hell now." Tori chuckled.

Honcho was the replica of Kilo. They both had smooth chocolate skin, deep waves, dimples and dark, dreamy eyes. He rubbed his stomach. "Shit, I been eating good on that financial aid money. On the flipside, school and football been beating my ass. But you know I'm still making straight A's and handling my business on the field."

"My nigga." Kilo dapped up his baby brother. "Make me proud."

"That's the plan. I had to take a break and come see my bro, though." Honcho hugged him again. "Damn, I missed you. I'm so happy to see you home."

"It's good to be back. I missed you too, lil bro, and I'm happy to see you doing good. Just stay focused and get that degree."

"Shidd, a nigga going to the NFL."

"Most definitely, but get that education. Do something different, you feel me?"

"Yeah, bro. We can chop it up later on that tip." Honcho rubbed his hands together. "Right now, I'm trying to get lit. Class ain't in session. I left my professors at Georgia Tech."

Kilo nodded his head. "Go enjoy yourself. Everything on me."

"Bet." Honcho stepped away and greeted the homies.

Tori placed her hand on Kilo's firm chest. "Baby, I'm going to find my girls. I'll be right back."

"A'ight." Kilo smacked her ass as she looked away. "I'm trying to make a baby tonight."

"We'll see." She giggled as she walked off.

Tori strutted through the club in a tight, fitted leather dress. It was hard to miss her womanly curves and thick thighs. Several dudes tried to get her attention, but she brushed them off with no hesitation, the same way she did while her man was on lock. Not a nigga on the planet can say he fucked or even caught a whiff of the pussy. Tori kept her legs closed and her heart on chill until Kilo touched down. He was her first and Tori made it her mission to make sure Kilo was the only one.

Tori spotted her girls standing by the bar, so she crept up on them unnoticed. "Hey whores," she shouted, once she was close enough.

"Hey slut." Tweety hugged her girl. Dazzle and Lala did the same.

"Y'all bought drinks already?" Tori asked.

"We about to. A bitch trying to get drunk and fucked tonight." Lala laughed, while sticking out her tongue.

"It's plenty of liquor in the VIP section. Keep y'all money."

"Well, if it's free, then it's for me." Lala was acting as if she already had a drink.

"Let's go so we can stop holding up the line." Tori prepared to leave.

"Hold up!" Dazzle held her hand up. "Who all over there?"

"Kilo, Fresh, Milo and Honcho."

Lala's ears perked up. "Honcho?"

"Yes girl, Honcho."

"Ooh, bitch, let's go. I need to see my baby." Lala was overly excited to see her old flame.

Tweety couldn't wait to jump in. "Girl, when was the last time you talked to that man?" Her tone was laced with bitterness. She always had a thing for Honcho, but he wanted Lala instead. At one point, Tweety thought she was the bombshell in the group, because she was the lightest. That was furthest from the truth because Honcho deflated all the air in her head. Just the mention of his name took her back to the day she overheard his comment about her. *"Tweety ain't dark enough for me. I'm trying to fuck with Lala pretty chocolate ass."*

"Doesn't matter. Honcho will always be my baby and I will always get that dick."

"I guess." Tweety tried to laugh it off like she was unbothered, but deep down she was still jealous of her friend.

"Dazzle, is the list up to par with you? Can we go now?" Tori asked.

"Yeah. I just want to vent to my girls, that's all," she sighed.

Tori grabbed her hand. "You still can. Those niggas too busy getting drunk to be paying us any attention."

The girls made their way back to where the fellas were hanging out at. A few dudes tried to pull Dazzle away for a dance, but she declined all offers.

Kilo spotted them coming through, so he met them halfway. "I see the gang is all here." He passed a new bottle of Patrón to Lala. "Drinks on me tonight, sis."

"Thanks, bro." Lala peeked over his shoulder. "Where's my baby?"

Kilo nodded in the opposite direction. "He over there. I'll send him over."

"Yeah, do that."

Tori, Dazzle, Lala and Tweety sat down on the sofa that was positioned in the corner. "What's up, sis? Why you in a pissy mood tonight? This is not like you."

"I need a drink first." Lala removed the seal from the bottle so they could pour up. Once their drinks were in hand, Dazzle finally spoke up. "Now remember earlier when I called you about Tron?"

"Yeah," Tori replied.

"I'm just tired of his ass. All he do is complain about my job and I'm sick of it. I make way more money than he does while he out there petty hustling."

Tweety couldn't wait to respond. She hated Tron with a passion and quite frankly, she was tired of hearing about their dysfunctional ass situationship. "Put his ass out. Send his ass back to his mama house. Problem solved," she laughed.

"Really, Tweety?" Tori hated Tweety's humor at times. It was funny that it conveniently came up at the wrong time.

"What? You thinking it too. I'm just the one who said it."

"Stop being so insensitive damn. They do have a baby together."

"You right. I'm sorry, Dazzle. I've been drinking. Ignore me." Tweety sat back and sipped on her drink in silence.

Tori sat quietly as Dazzle vented about no-good-ass Tron. She went into every detail about the events that led up to her funky mood. "So, y'all were fighting in front of my godson?"

"I mean, briefly. We stopped when we heard him crying."

"You need to figure out what you gone do. That's not healthy. I'm not going to tell you to leave him, because I know how it feels when people are against the one you love. All I can say is do what's best for you and Jamir."

"This is so hard for me."

"Whatever you need, let me know. I got you. I promise. It doesn't matter what—" Tori stopped mid-sentence. Her attention was on Tweety, who had her nose tooted up like she smelled an old period pad. Out of curiosity, she looked behind her and saw Lala sitting in Honcho's lap. Tori wasn't a fool by a long shot, but she decided to address the situation later and continue with her conversation.

"It doesn't matter what it is. I got you both."

"Thanks, Tori." They hugged it out.

The music stopped abruptly. They heard a heated argument. Tori immediately jumped up to make sure it wasn't Kilo. Gunshots rang out loudly throughout the club.

Boc! Boc! Boc! Boc!

Tori dropped to the ground, but she could hear her name being called. "Tori! Tori!" When she finally looked up, she was being picked up by Kilo. "Baby, you okay?"

Tori didn't speak. She just nodded her head.

"I got you. Come on."

Kilo and his boys made sure the girls were okay before they made a run for it. No one had a gun on them, so they had to move with caution, although they had a feeling the gunmen were long gone. The crowd was moving fast, trying to make it to their cars. Kilo held onto Tori for dear life, as they rushed through the door to safety.

*****

Inside the car, Tori sat in silence and looked out the window. Kilo grabbed her hand and held it. "You okay, baby?"

"Yeah."

"You sure?" He knew better than to believe that.

"When I heard those shots, all I could think about was you. I was so scared."

"Come here." Tori slid to the middle of the seat. Kilo put his arm around her. "Don't be scared, baby. You know I can hold my own."

"I know, but look at what happened. You left your gun in the car. This could've played out so much differently."

"Ain't nobody gunning for me baby."

"Bullets don't have a name."

"You right." Kilo kissed her forehead. His cellphone vibrated inside his pocket, so Tori moved slightly to the left so he could remove it.

"Yo," Kilo answered. Tori laid her head back down.

"You and sis good?" Honcho asked.

"Yeah, we good. Make sure her girls get home safe."

"I got 'em, bro."

"Thanks, bro, hit me up when you make it home."

"I'll hit you when I get to Lala's crib. I'm not going home tonight."

"I should've known. Be safe." Kilo chuckled.

"I will," he chuckled, before ending the call. Kilo passed the phone to Tori, so he could focus on the road.

Kilo and Tori arrived at the hotel close to two o'clock. Tori's mind was still racing and sex was the furthest thing from her mind. All she wanted to do was lay down and forget about that night's events. Removing her clothes, she crawled underneath the blanket. Kilo stripped down to his boxers and joined her.

"Can you just hold me? I don't want to do anything else."

"We don't have to." Kilo pulled her close.

Tori felt safe in his arms, so she was able to get comfortable right away. "Get some sleep, baby." Tori closed her eyes and draped her arm across his chest. She latched onto him tightly until she fell asleep to the beat of his heart.

Chapter 3

The weekend breezed by quickly and Monday morning wasted no time showing up. That meant back to business for Tori. The house was eerily quiet when she made it inside. Normally, the squad was there for their early morning meeting. Tori clutched her overnight bag in her hand, as she proceeded up the steps.

"Tori Price!" Diesel shouted.

"Yes."

"Get in here."

Tori sucked her teeth and descending down the stairwell. In her gut, she knew the conversation wasn't about to be a pleasant one. That was the only time he called out her whole name. She just hoped it had nothing to do with Kilo, although she knew better. Diesel was sitting at the table sipping from a coffee mug.

"Yes."

"Have a seat. We need to talk."

That was confirmation a lecture was coming. Diesel took a sip from his mug and sat it down in front of him. "About what?"

"Do you remember that talk we had one year ago at this very table?" he quizzed.

"Yeah, I do."

"So, when are you leaving? I've been waiting on you to give me a date and nothing has come my way. None of your clothes are packed and I don't see any boxes around here either."

Tori looked down at the floor and twiddled her fingers. She was trying to stall him out. Her mind was already made up. All she needed was her mouth to follow suit.

"Tori, you need to answer me."

After remaining quiet for another minute, she slowly rose her head. Their eyes locked and her heart began to beat hard against her chest. "I'm not leaving."

A huge vein protruded across Diesel's forehead. That was a clear indication her father was livid. To Tori's surprise he remained calm, but his voice was stern. "You decided to stay where? Not in this house."

"Yes."

"Absolutely not. One year ago today, you promised me that if I allowed you to take one year off from school and hustle, you will go. That was the agreement."

Tori didn't want to break his heart, but it had to be done. "I'm sorry, Dad, but I no longer have the desire to go to college. I want to stay here and up my rank in the organization and eventually start my own thing."

Diesel was beyond disappointment with his child. In fact he was infuriated with her decision. "Tori, this is not the plan or dream I envisioned for you."

"How so?" She folded her arms across her chest.

"I always wanted you to have a better life than this," he pleaded.

Tori looked around and smiled. "Take a look at how we live. No degree will ever put me in a position to live like this. I'm accustomed to this life and you made sure of it."

"So, what you're saying is you want to be a part of the same organization and sell the same exact drug that took your mother away?"

The sudden reminder of her mother struck her in the chest, knocking the wind out of her lungs. A slew of tears flooded her eye lids and streamed down her cheeks. Bianca's death was still painful, as if it happened yesterday. Diesel quickly regretted his harsh comment. "Tori, I'm sorry, baby. I didn't mean that."

Tori was enraged with anger and it was too late to apologize. "Yes, you did. So, don't apologize. You didn't love my mother. I can tell by the way you treated her."

Diesel rubbed his head. His daughter's accusations were far from the truth, but at that time she was too young to understand. As far as he was concerned, she was still too young. The last thing he wanted to do was tarnish the memory of her.

"Tori, there are some things in life you will never understand. One of them is the marriage between your mother and me. It was difficult to say the least, but I loved her more than you could ever know. If I could change anything about the past, I would. So, don't ever forget that. Me and your mother been together since we were teenagers. She was my first love. She gave me my first child. Bianca will always hold a special place in my heart."

"You didn't act like it. I thought you hated her. I'll never forget the way you treated her on my sixteenth birthday."

Diesel stood up and walked to the other end of the table. The sight of his baby girl crying wasn't sitting well with him. Gently, he grabbed her arm and pulled her from the chair. Diesel held her tight. "In death, I love your mother and that's the God's honest truth. Bianca was sick and I had a temper, so that equaled a bad combination. Should I have been gentle with her? Yes. She knew what buttons to push and I allowed her to get the best of me. If I could take back what I did to her, I would."

Tori wiped her eyes and looked up in her father's face. "What did you do to her?"

Diesel realized he said too much and he needed to clean up his response. "I didn't protect her from herself. Bianca was my wife and I shouldn't have let her get so far gone. I didn't help her the way I should've."

"I miss her so much, Daddy." Tori placed her head on his chest and cried. Diesel felt that guilt grip his neck, as he looked up at the ceiling and shed a few tears of his own. He would die before he let the truth come out about Bianca.

***

A few hours had passed. Tori decided to get out the house and get up with her girls. She needed to clear her head and discuss a business opportunity with them. Lala sat in the passenger seat giggling and texting. Tori turned the volume down on the stereo.

"Bitch, who got you skinning and grinning over there?"

"You already know." Lala's eyes never left the screen.

"That must be Honcho."

"Fuck yeah."

"Damn, I see he put it down all weekend."

Lala finally looked up with a huge smile on her face. "Girl, yes. That young man beat my pussy into submission. Now I see why you so submissive to Kilo's ass."

Tori blushed at the thought of her man laying it down. "What can I say? That fresh-out dick ain't shit to play with. I'm so hooked that I can't see another nigga."

"See, that's what I'm saying. He got a bitch dickmatized. It wasn't like this when we first started fucking back then." Lala patted her thigh. "Woo! Honcho must've been studying porn or taking classes."

Tori busted out into a fit of laughter. "Girl, you dumb. What damn classes he took? Sex education?"

"I don't know, but whatever it was I'm loving it."

"That man hit you with some grown dick, that's all."

"Shit, I felt that grown dick, so I know."

Tori pulled up in the gated community where Dazzle lived and parked. As she silenced the engine, the two women emerged from the car. The sun was setting on the horizon. Quietly, they walked down the hall until they reached her door. Tori knocked and waited patiently. Dazzle answered the door with the quickness. Apparently, she had been waiting hours on their arrival.

"Damn, took y'all long enough."

"Girl, you know how we do." Tori placed her hand on her hip. "Where is raggedy ass Tron?"

The mention of his name made Dazzle roll her eyes. "Probably out with his Monday bitch," she stated with conviction.

Lala brushed past Dazzle with her hand raised high in the air. "And yet and still, you stay. Just get out of this fucked-up situation and take that loss. You tried and it didn't work."

Tori sat down beside Lala and crossed her legs. "I have to say I agree with her. All this nigga doing is holding you back."

"I know. I just hate to take my baby away from his daddy." Dazzle knew she deserved better, but it was harder to leave when a child was involved. "My baby is used to waking up to his mama and daddy."

Tori hated to overstep her boundaries when it came to her girls' relationships, but clearly her advice was needed. "Dazzle, I hate to sound harsh, but it sounds like you're just using Jamir as an excuse to stay with him. It's like you're trying to find a reason to keep him around and that's crazy to me. He ain't bringing shit to the table, so you ain't losing shit but some in-house dick. But guess what? It's plenty of niggas out here that's willing to pay bills. Stop letting this nigga use you."

Dazzle took every word she said to heart. Opinions only hurt when the truth was attached. Tori was right about everything and there was no point in trying to defend her reasoning. Granted, it wasn't what she wanted to hear. It was what she needed to hear. After digesting those painful words, Dazzle decided to reply.

"You're right. I do need to let him go. It's just so hard. I don't feel like learning a new person all over again and starting over."

Lala sucked her teeth. She had enough of the bullshit excuses. "Girl, bye. You don't know the nigga you currently laying with. This nigga turned into a brand-new bitch."

Dazzle sighed and ran her hand through her braids. "Okay, I get it. I just need to put some shit in order."

Tori didn't want to spend any more valuable time discussing sorry ass Tron. "I'm not judging you. Take your time. I'll be here for whatever you decide. But on a more important note, I need to know if y'all trying to make some money?"

Lala's ears perked up. "Make money how?"

Tori wasn't sure on how they would react, but it was now or never. "Well, as y'all know, I'm working for Diesel."

Lala jumped right in. "You mean your daddy, girl?"

"Duh! How many Diesel's do you know?" Tori replied snappily.

"Duh, my ass. You could've just said your daddy from the jump."

"Bitch, shut up!" Tori fussed.

"Yeah, shut up, cause a bitch about to be a single parent and I need extra money."

Lala laughed. "You been a single parent." Dazzle shot her a bird.

Tori continued with her pitch. "So, y'all already know I'm not going to college. I've decided to stay here and build my own empire. Me and Diesel," Tori paused and cut her eyes at Lala. "My father and I had an argument earlier about my decision. I know he's going to cut me off soon, so I need to get my own shit up and running. But of course, I need a team. Most importantly, I need people I can trust."

The living room got quiet for a second. However, that was short lived when Jamir entered the room with a face full of fresh tears. "Mommy," he cried.

"Come here, baby." Dazzle reached out for her son.

"Come to me, Goddie Jamir." The toddler stopped in his tracks and rubbed his eyes. When he saw Tori, he quickly changed routes and went to his godmother. Once he quieted down, Tori went back to the conversation. "On a serious note, I want to put this game in the chokehold and I know I can do it."

Dazzle was definitely interested in a career change. Her number-one goal was to create a lifestyle for Jamir. Living hand to mouth was no longer an option. "Well, I'm down. Just tell me what I need to do."

"Good." Tori looked at Lala. "What about you?"

Lala was a bit skeptical, but she always wanted to live the same lifestyle as Tori. "Count me in, shit."

"I knew I could count on y'all."

"Did you ask Tweety?" Lala questioned.

"No. I haven't spoken to her about it yet. When I called, she didn't answer."

"Oh, well, she might be at work." Lala suggested.

"Nah. She off on Mondays." Tori fished her phone out of her purse and called her once more. Then she sat it down on the sofa. "She didn't answer."

"That hoe always missing on Mondays. Acting like she busy, with her jealous ass." Lala tooted up her nose.

"Why you say that?" The comment piqued Tori's interest.

"I saw how she was looking at me and Honcho in the club. She wanna fuck him so bad."

"Yeah, I peeped that too." Dazzle stood up. "I need a drink. How about y'all?"

"Fuck, yeah. Pour that shit up." Lala stood up and followed Dazzle into the kitchen.

Tori's phone started to ring. When she looked down at the screen, she saw Tweety was calling back. "Hello." There was no response. "Hello." The sound of rustling could be heard. "Tweety!" Tori shouted. Still nothing. Instead of hanging up, she waited a moment to see if she would respond. After waiting a few seconds longer, she heard moaning and heavy grunting. Tori continued to listen and knew Tweety was someplace getting her back knocked out, so she hung up.

Both girls walked back into the room. Lala handed Tori a glass before taking a seat. "Tweety just called me back."

"What did she say?" Dazzle asked out of curiosity.

"She didn't say anything, because she's too busy getting fucked right now."

Lala choked on her drink. "What?"

"Her phone dialed me by accident. I could hear her having sex in the background."

"Eww! With who?" Dazzle sipped her drink.

"I have no idea." Tori sipped her drink. "Within the next couple of weeks, I'll have everything up and running. I'm going to sit down and have a talk with Kilo. With me and him working as a team, I know we can have the drug game on lock. He's feared in the streets and that's what we're going to need, in order to run a smooth operation. I'm a female and I know they gone try me."

"They ain't gone try you once they know you belong to Kilo," Lala stated matter-of-factly.

"What about your daddy though?" Dazzle quickly brought Tori back to reality.

"I'm grown and he can't tell me who to date."

"Yeah, that's why y'all still creeping." Dazzle giggled.

"Not for long. He's going to find out very soon. I'm tired of keeping our love a secret." Tori sat her drink down and laid Jamir on the sofa. Within the next month or so, she was going to leave Diesel's house for good and there was going to be no turning back.

Chapter 4

Diesel pulled up in the secluded Weston neighborhood and parked in the driveway of his second home. Four years ago, he purchased the home and never told a soul. Not even Bianca. True enough, he loved his wife, but their marriage was over in his eyes. Therefore, he'd kept his secret up until that day.

The house was brightly lit and he could see movement through the front window. Diesel tucked his gun in his lower back and unlocked the door. His presence was unknown until he closed the door and locked it. That was the moment a small figure ran towards him.

"Daddy! Daddy!"

Diesel swooped his son up into his arms and kissed his cheek. "What's up, lil man? I missed you."

"Did you miss me?" Jenna stepped up to him and placed her arm around his waist.

"Of course, I did." He then placed a kiss on her soft pink lips.

"So, what took you so long to show up? It's been a whole week," Jenna complained.

"Shit has been crazy, but I'm here now."

"Yeah, but for how long?" Jenna folded her arms across her chest.

"What you trippin' for? Damn, I'm here." He walked over to the sofa and sat down with his son on his lap.

"Me estoy hartando de esta mierda. Será mejor que reúnas tus cosas antes de que me vaya para siempre esta vez," she shouted.

Diesel looked up at her with an unsettling look on his face. "What I told you about speaking that shit to me? Speak English, goddammit."

"I said, I'm getting sick of this shit. You better get your shit together before I leave for good this time," Jenna repeated herself.

The last thing he wanted to do was have an argument with the mother of his child in front of their son. Diesel stood up and left Jenna standing in the living room. He then opened his son's bedroom door and walked inside. The room was extremely dark, so he turned on the light and headed over to the racecar bed. Gently, he laid his namesake Torin Price Jr., down and tucked him in.

"Daddy, can you read me a bedtime story?"

"Sure. Let me grab a book." Diesel went over to the bookshelf and grabbed *Goldilocks and the Three Bears*, which was Torin's favorite book.

Diesel sat on the edge of the bed and got comfortable. As he read the book to his young prince, he constantly stared at the similar features the two shared. Torin Jr., was a much lighter version of his father, due to the fact that his mother was Puerto Rican. His hair was dark and curly, and his eyes were wide and brown. He truly loved his son and wanted to see him every single day. But the fact that Tori was unaware of his existence made it that much harder. Eventually, he knew he would have to tell the truth.

Junior was knocked out halfway through the story. Diesel closed the book and kissed his baby boy on the forehead. "I love you so much, son, and one day you are going to meet your sister. I just have to wait for the right time."

Diesel stood up and when he turned around, Jenna was standing at the door with her hands on her hips. "I've heard that same lie for four years now and nothing has changed." Then she walked away.

In his heart, he knew she had every right to be upset. He had promised to come clean about his indiscretion long before Bianca passed away. The main problem now was Tori. He knew his daughter would have zero understanding about his secret life.

Jenna was sitting in the kitchen drinking a glass of wine when he walked in. "How much longer do you plan to hide me and your son from your daughter?"

"As long as it takes for her to understand. The timing has to be right. I thought she would've been off to college by now, but now she doesn't want to leave."

"That sounds like a 'you' problem, Diesel. I've been quiet long enough. I've been living in this house alone and I'm tired of it. I deserve to be happy. I deserve to have a man that wants to be with me and it's obvious you don't want the same thing."

Diesel walked up to her and stood beside her. Slowly, he raised his hand and caressed her cheek. "You know how I feel about you. You also know how I feel about my daughter. This is not something I can just spring on her."

"Our son is about to be four. Don't you think it's time to tell the truth? Bianca has been dead for three years now. You told me she was the only problem. Not your daughter. If she loves you, she'll understand."

"I know what I said," Diesel sighed and rubbed his head. "Just give me a little more time. I'll tell her soon. I promise."

"I've heard that before." Jenna shifted her body on the stool to put some distance between them. Then she grabbed the wine bottle and refilled her glass.

"You have no patience."

The wine glass resting on her lips had now found its way on the marble countertop. "Patience? Don't you dare talk to me about patience, when I've been living in this hellhole for far too long. You've been controlling me the whole time and my dumb ass still here. I allowed you to move me out west with no transportation and no access to anything or anyone close."

"You don't need transportation. That's what my driver is for. Does he or does he not take you where you need to go?"

"That's surveillance. Just another way to keep me at bay and silent." Jenna began to shed tears. "One thing is clear to me, you don't love me the way I love you."

"That's a lie. I do love you," he stated truthfully.

"No, you don't." Jenna took a sip of her drink. "I'm sorry, but I'm moving on. I need love and it's obvious I'll never get that from you."

Diesel grabbed the bridge of his nose and took a deep breath. Truthfully speaking, he knew the day would come when she would feel that. However, that wasn't happening. His eyes met hers. "If you think you going anywhere, you have another thing coming."

"What do I have coming?"

His big, brown eyes turned into tiny slits. "Do you think I would let you leave me?"

"You don't own me or my pussy. I can do what I want." Jenna continued to test him.

Swiftly, Diesel grabbed the back of her neck and squeezed it. "I will kill you if I even think you fucking another man. You and this pussy belongs to me and me only. Don't get it twisted."

Jenna was instantly turned on by his aggression. It was impossible to stay mad at him. Instead of arguing with him, she swiveled the chair in his direction and looked into his eyes. Her hands made their way to the crotch of his pants. Gently, she caressed his piece. Diesel leaned down and tongue kissed her. Aggressively, he snatched her from the counter and pulled down her tights.

The passion in the air was thick as train smoke. Diesel lifted her up on the counter and pushed her legs apart. The sight of her olive-colored kitty turned him on. It had been a while, so his appetite was heavy. Hungrily, he feasted on her goodies. Jenna was so caught up in his whirlwind, she had forgotten about being upset not even five minutes ago. The warmth of his tongue slithering between her folds had her on edge.

Diesel used his right hand to unbuckle his jeans. Once his piece was free, he raised up and dipped inside her warm twat. Gripping her light-colored cheeks, he slammed inside her repeatedly.

"I missed you so much," she moaned.

"I know you did," he grunted, while using his pent-up anger to murder her kitty. Diesel placed his hand around her throat and kissed her. "Give my shit away and I'll kill you. I promise you that."

"I won't. I. Promise."

Diesel hammered Jenna down until he busted inside her tummy. Afterwards, he carried her to the bedroom to do it all over again. When he was done, Jenna laid on her stomach and cuddled up underneath him.

"Why can't I have this every night? This is all I want."

"What? Some dick."

"No. Not just that. I want you. Our son deserves to wake up to both of his parents every morning. The same way you did with your daughter. Don't you think that's fair?"

Diesel couldn't deny he felt the same way, but he was too worried about damaging his relationship with Tori. "I'm going to work on it."

"After you tell her, are you going to move out here with us? I'm not moving into the house you shared with your wife. This is our home. I love it here, but you're the only thing missing."

"I got you and my son."

"I hope so. We need you, baby."

"I know, baby."

"I love you."

"I love you too."

Jenna fingered the two-carat diamond rock on her left hand. "Are we still getting married?"

"Yes. Once the smoke clears, we'll get married."

"You promise?"

"I do."

Diesel laid in bed, staring up at the ceiling while Jenna slept peacefully. The idea of coming clean was really tugging at his heart. A feeling deep down in his gut told him he was about to lose the most important woman in his life. At that point, he didn't know what to do. Ultimately, he thought he had more time, but now he felt defeated. The secret he was holding felt like an anchor and Diesel desperately wanted to come clean.

***

The following morning, Tori woke up to bright sunrays beaming in her face. A huge yawn escaped her lips as she rubbed her eyes. Kilo's side of the bed was empty and cold. Tori sat up and slid from underneath the blanket. After leaving Dazzle's apartment, she'd made her way to her man and for the majority of the night they discussed business. When that was done, Kilo used the rest of his energy trying to plant his seed.

Tori picked up her clothes from the floor and got dressed before going to use the bathroom and brush her teeth. Once her hygiene was in check, she left the room and went downstairs to find Kilo. To her surprise, Kilo was in the living room, sitting with Eazy and Honcho.

"Good morning, sleepy head." Kilo smiled.

"Hey, baby. Good morning, everybody." Eazy and Honcho said their good mornings.

Kilo approached her and kissed her lips. "How did you sleep?"

"Like a baby, but I think you knew that already."

Kilo laughed. "Yeah. Put that ass to bed."

Tori slapped his arm. "Be quiet."

"It's okay, sis. I heard y'all nasty asses," Honcho chuckled.

Tori covered her face. "Oh my goodness, I'm so embarrassed."

"I kept telling you to be quiet."

"Come walk me outside. Bye y'all."

"See ya later," Honcho and Eazy replied.

Kilo escorted Tori to her car. Leaning against the door, he pulled her close. "I spoke to my dad about the business. He's willing to introduce us to his connect, but we have to be serious about going to the top."

"Oh, I'm very serious. This is my calling. You see how I operate."

"I need you to be sure about this."

"I'm very sure. I can do this." Tori grabbed both of his hands. "We can do this."

"Let me find out my baby wants to be a certified trap queen."

"I do," she smiled. "And you will be my trap king." They kissed once more and then Tori was on her way.

Twenty-five minutes later, Tori pulled up in her driveway. Not even a minute later, Diesel was pulling in right behind her. Stepping outside the car, her father approached her.

"Good morning." Diesel kissed her forehead.

"Good morning. Where you coming from?" she quizzed.

"On an errand." The lie rolled off his tongue smoothly. "Come inside. We need to talk." Tori strolled behind him without the slightest idea about what was to come next.

Chapter 5
Two weeks later

Tori put on her jewelry to add the final touches to her Camilla and Marc satin jumpsuit. Then she slipped her feet into a pair of black pumps. Kilo grabbed her waist from behind and planted a kiss on her neck. "You look beautiful."

"Thank you, baby." Tori turned to face him. "And you look handsome."

"You ready to go handle this business?"

"I'm more than ready."

"Good. Let's ride."

Kilo grabbed Tori's hand and escorted her out the room and down the stairs. Eazy was sitting on the sofa, flipping through channels on the television when they walked in. "We out, Pops."

Eazy looked down at his watch, then back up to his son with a smile like a proud father. "Being early is important. You never want to be late when dealing with a man of his stature. His time is valuable, so be respectful."

"We got this. The meeting starts in one hour."

"Good luck."

"I got my good luck charm right here." Kilo dapped up his father and they left the house.

On their way to meet the plug, Kilo schooled her. "When we get here, let me do all the talking, except when he's talking to you. This nigga in the big league, so bring that A-game you possess."

"You have nothing to worry about, baby. I was born to do this shit." Tori crossed her legs. "Besides, this is the moment I've been waiting for."

"That's my girl." Kilo took his eyes off the road for a quick second and pop kissed her on the lips. "Sexy ass."

Kilo had the ability to make any woman feel special, but one would never find out because Tori had staked her claim. A huge smile was plastered across her lips. She grabbed his hand and intertwined her fingers with his. "I love you so much, baby."

"I love you too."

The remainder of their forty-minute ride was done in silence. As Kilo whipped into the Coral Gables neighborhood, they were greeted by big, beautiful palm trees. Every house they passed was bigger and more lavish than the first.

Finally, they reached a dead end that held the biggest house on the block. It was surrounded by a black, iron fence. "This nigga living like Al Pacino." Tori exhaled, while taking in the breathtaking view.

"This shit looks like the White House."

"This is how I want to live. Me, you and our three kids."

"Oh, I was thinking five."

"You can get whatever you want."

Kilo stopped at the security post and rolled down the window. "I'm here to see the boss."

"Go right in, he's expecting you."

Kilo pushed past the booth and cruised up the driveway. The BMW came to a complete stop and he opened the door. Kilo stepped over to the passenger side and opened the door. Broward County's finest couple hit the pavement like they were on the red carpet at the *Grammy Awards*. Just as they stepped onto the porch, the door swung open and there stood a brown-skinned, older man wearing a gold satin robe.

"Little Eazy, boy, you look just like your daddy," he laughed, while extending his arm for a handshake.

Kilo did the same. "I prefer Kilo. I'm walking in my own footsteps."

"That you are." Domino's attention landed on the beautiful bombshell standing beside his potential new distributor. Gently, he grabbed her hand and kissed it. "You are absolutely gorgeous."

"Thank you."

Kilo separated Domino and Tori's hands. "You trying to steal my lady right in front of me, huh?" He joked, but with a serious tone.

"I'm just admiring your impeccable taste in women. No disrespect intended."

"None taken. Now can we go inside and talk business?"

"Sure thing, let's go." Domino trailed in behind them and closed the door.

In the living room, there were twelve half-naked women chatting and laughing like they were fully clothed. Domino clapped his hands twice. The noise in the room stopped immediately. "Welcome to my stable." He turned and smiled at Kilo. "Stand up, ladies."

They all did like they were told. Each female was a different shade of chocolate, caramel and vanilla.

"These are my big, fine stallions." He rubbed his hands together and licked his lips. "Ladies, meet my associates Kilo and his lady, Tori. We have business to discuss, so I need you to return to your rooms until I call for you."

"Yes, Daddy," they sang in harmony.

Domino introduced every female by their pet name, as they walked pass him and kissed his cheek. Kilo and Tori were slightly amused. The line grew smaller. "And this is my Arabian horse, Brazilian, Spanish and Puerto Rican horse." The room was finally empty.

"Have a seat." He extended his arm and pointed to the sofa across from him.

Tori sat down first and crossed her legs. Kilo adjusted his blazer before sitting beside her. Ready to discuss business, he leaned forward and folded his hands. "I appreciate you seeing me and my lady on short notice. I know how busy you are."

Domino sat back and placed his elbows on the arm of the plush chair. "No problem. When your father hit me up and explained everything to me, I knew I had to see you. Well, the both of you actually. So Tori, you're Diesel's daughter, huh?"

"Yes. I am."

"I hate to pry, but why not cop work from your father, so you can get your bricks at a cheaper rate?"

Family business wasn't what she intended on speaking about. Two weeks ago, her father cut her off for declining college. Yet and still, she would never expose their business. It almost felt as though he was indeed prying. Whatever she and Diesel had going on was a private matter, with exception to Kilo. It was something not intended for outsiders to know. The last thing she needed was anyone thinking it was okay to make a move or try some shit.

"We all know family, business and money doesn't mix. Therefore, I'm looking to start up my own organization with the help of my better half." Tori kept a straight face. "I've worked for my father for the past year, but I want more."

"Is that right?" Domino was curious.

"Indeed."

"So, do you have your own territory? Or, are you looking to take over?"

"That would be a Kilo question. However, I do have a team in place already. They've been working for me since I started."

"I'm impressed. It sounds like you know what you're doing."

"I do."

"Now, Kilo. Can you guarantee that I have a secure pipeline with you and the Mrs.? The last thing I need is to lose money. That won't be good for either of us."

Kilo looked Domino in the eyes. "You have my word. This operation will run smooth like Dunkin Donuts during the morning work rush. I'm highly respected in the streets and I'm smart, so your product is in good hands."

"I hope so." Domino stood up and shook their hands. "I am willing to take a chance on both of you. Please don't disappoint me."

"We won't," Kilo assured him.

"Great! Follow me to the kitchen for a drink. Then we can talk numbers." Kilo held Tori's hand and followed Domino. Tori was extremely happy, but she kept her composure and remained professional. Things were finally going her way and she couldn't be happier.

***

Oakland Park, FL

Trap House / Delivery Day

"Whew! It's looking like Christmas around this bitch." Kilo laughed while removing the bricks of cocaine from the coffee barrel Domino had delivered. He placed them all on the table, one by one. Tori's eyes lit up. She couldn't believe it was finally happening.

Picking up one of the bricks, she examined it. "Santa came early, baby."

Kilo placed the last brick on the table. "Alright, now there are twenty-five bricks total. What's the street value?"

Tori thought quickly about her response. "We can make an easy half a mill off of this. If we selling them for twenty a piece."

"True indeed, but not everyone is going to purchase a whole brick. That means we can't forget about our corner boys. Also, remember there is competition out here. We have the best coke hands down, but we need to have the best prices too. Once we snatch them up, we can go up on the price. But, Domino is cutting us a sweet deal, so it's a win for us either way."

"Okay, I get what you're saying." Tori nodded her head. "That makes sense."

"My boys will be copping from us from now on and they only grabbing bricks. We should be able to off these bricks quick and after that, Domino will automatically up our product to fifty bricks. That's when we'll start seeing real money."

"I have a few niggas that grab bricks only. Everyone else gets ounces and sometimes halves. We can definitely get rid of this in a week," Tori added.

"No doubt about that."

Tori sat down on the stool and massaged her temple. "I have to find a place soon."

"You don't have to rush and do that. Pops cool with you living there. He loves you like a daughter."

"So does Diesel and look what happened."

"That's because he doesn't accept you for who and what you are. Eazy knows what time it is and he'll never do that to you. He loves the company. One thing about it, my father always wanted a big family."

Tori looked into his eyes. "What happened with that? It's only two of y'all."

"My mom didn't want to have any more kids after she had Honcho. Her pregnancy was high risk with him. I watched her go through it. After that, she told my father she was done." Kilo thought back to the countless fights his parents had every day of the week. "They used to fight all the time after that. My father even started to cheat on her with some woman. She couldn't handle it and that's how she ended up in prison."

"What happened?" As long as she'd known Kilo, the truth about his mother was never revealed.

"She attacked a pregnant woman. The lady lost her baby. She was charged with aggravated assault and manslaughter for the baby."

"Damn, that's crazy." Tori placed her hand on his cheek and rubbed her nose against his. "That'll be me, so you better not cheat on me."

"I'll never do that." Kilo grabbed her hand and kissed her knuckles. "I love you too much for that."

"I love you more than life itself," she admitted. Their lips locked and the two engaged in a slow, passionate kiss. Tori opened her legs and pulled him closer. "Make love to me now," she whispered.

Kilo lifted her from the chair, carried her over to the sectional sofa and laid her down. Tori was anxious to feel his touch, so she removed her clothes quickly and tossed them onto the floor. Kilo stripped down as well. Standing in front of her, he stroked his semi-stiff rod, as he looked into her brown eyes.

Tori was turned on instantly. Seduction was heavy in the air like thick weed smoke. With her back against the pillows, she spread her legs, placed two of her fingers onto her clit and caressed her hardening bud. "I need it right now." Tori licked her lips while looking into his eyes and fingering herself.

"I'mma handle my pussy. Move your hand." Kilo grabbed both of her legs and pulled her closer to him. Her back was on the cushion and her ass hung off freely. Holding her cheeks, he plunged his soldier into her wet goodies. The tightness of her pussy suctioned the head when he pulled back a little. "Grrr!" he grunted in satisfaction, then going deeper.

Tori enjoyed every stroke, while thrusting her hips towards his pelvis. "Ah! Yes! Yes! Just like that."

Kilo held the back of the sofa and pounded the wetness out of her juice box. Tori placed her hand on his abs and closed her eyes. The pressure of his length pressing against her stomach was filled with pleasurable pain.

"Ah! Ahhh! Fuck," she screamed.

"Who pussy this is?"

"Yours, baby."

"Scoot back." Kilo grabbed Tori's ankles and pushed them against the back of the sofa. The trip back into her guts was better than the first time. Tori's sex faces turned him on, while he rammed his piece in and out. "Shit!" The sound of their skin smacking filled the room.

Kilo flipped Tori over and committed a one-eighty-seven on the pussy. Gripping her hips, he beat her from the back at a fast pace. Tori's hands gripped the hell out of the pillow cushions, as she bit down on her bottom lip.

"Yeah! Yes! Yess! Ouuu! Ahh!" she cried out. "Go deeper!"

"Cum for daddy," he demanded.

Kilo was in complete control and Tori was at his mercy. He wasn't stopping until she busted a nut first. To take things up a notch, he spread her cheeks and spit down her crack. His thumb made its way to the opening of her asshole. Slowly, he pushed it inside repeatedly.

"Make me cum! Make your pussy cum!" Tori begged.

"Hold your leg up." She did.

Kilo held both of her wrists to the middle of her back and hit her spot aggressively for several minutes. Eventually, she submitted his power and released a heavy load onto his dick. "I'm cumming! I'm cumming! Fuuuck!"

After a nice release, she eased from his grip while he was still standing and dropped to her knees. Tori grabbed his soaked piece of chocolate steel and slipped it into her mouth. She slurped hard, while bobbing up and down on her Snickers bar. Kilo grabbed a hand full of her naturally long hair, while thrusting his hips forward. Tori had grown accustomed to his massive monster hitting her tonsils, so her gag reflexes were at a minimum. Like a pro, she gobbled him up like a Thanksgiving dinner.

"Suck that dick. Drain that dick." Kilo massaged the life out of her scalp.

Tori opened her eyes while pleasing the love of her life. She needed to see the happy expression on his face. "Mm. Mm." His juices were sweet as they trickled down her throat. *Apparently, someone had been eating their fruit*, she thought.

Kilo's body trembled beneath her small hands. The build-up of his nut in his scrotum sack was beginning to get intense. That caused him to become a little aggressive with his strokes.

"Be still."

Kilo could feel himself about to let loose. While inhaling, he took a deep breath and looked down at her beautiful face. The sight of his wood covered with her spit made his knees buckle. The two locked eyes. "Open your mouth," he demanded in a low voice.

Kilo jacked his dick until he was shooting off into her mouth. When he was done, he shook off the remaining juices and Tori licked him clean. As she rose to her feet, Kilo placed his hand underneath her chin and kissed her in the mouth. "I'm going to marry you one day."

Kilo grabbed her hand and escorted her to the bedroom for round two. It was going to be a very long, exhausting night, so he placed a delivery order for food and liquor through one of his closest comrades.

Chapter 6
The next day

It was Monday morning and the candy shop was officially up and running. Tori stood at the bathroom sink brushing her teeth. The sound of the doorbell chimed through the house.

"I got it," Kilo shouted, while pulling a tank top over his head. As he got closer to the door, he heard heavy knocking. "I'm coming, muthafucka!"

Kilo pushed the door open to find his homie, Fresh, standing there smoking a blunt with a goofy grin on his face. "Took your ass long enough, nigga."

"I had to put on some clothes." Kilo closed the door and locked it.

"Hmm. Where's sis?" Fresh looked around the room.

"She back there." He nodded towards the hallway.

"Fuck y'all was doing? Getting a quickie in before the meeting?"

"Mind ya business, nigga."

"Whatever, nigga." Fresh sat down on the stool and faced Kilo. "Where is everybody else? I'm the only muthafucka that's here early."

"They on the way. Sit back, smoke your blunt and chill. I'll be right back."

Kilo left his boy alone and went to find Tori. When he walked into the bedroom, she was standing there in a robe. "Hurry up and get dressed. Fresh is here."

"Okay, baby." Tori pecked his lips. "I'll be out as soon as my girls get here. You can chat with your boy in peace."

"A'ight." Kilo smacked her on the ass. "Make sure you cover up too."

"Don't I always?"

"I'm just saying." Kilo left the room and closed the door behind him.

Thirty minutes later, the doorbell rang again. Tori knew it was her girls, so she joined them in the living room. On her way out, she was greeted with hugs and smiles from Dazzle and Lala.

"Wassup, bitch!" Dazzle laughed.

"Shit! Ready to run this check up." Tori was happy she had the support of two of her closest friends.

"So, where is your broke best friend?" Lala giggled, while looking around.

"Hell if I know. She act like she too scared to make money, so I'm not going to force it."

"Watch she try to jump on board when she see us thumbing through a check," Dazzle added.

"Right!" Tori extended her arm towards the kitchen. "Anyway, let's get to work. We don't have time to worry about her. Tweety has her own agenda on her off day, so let her be."

"You know I don't care about that hating ass bitch." Lala followed Tori into the kitchen.

Kilo and Fresh was standing around the kitchen table engaged in a conversation, but it stopped once they walked in. Fresh smiled when he saw Dazzle. "What's up, beautiful?"

"Aht! Aht! I appreciate the compliment, but I'm off limits." Lala brushed him off.

"Now you know damn well I wasn't talking to you." Fresh moved closer to Dazzle and licked his lips. "I'm talking to Dazzle thick ass."

"Fresh, back it up." Dazzle placed her hand on his chest. "I'm not interested in being nobody's side chick."

"What you talkin' about? I'm single as a dollar bill."

"For how long? I don't need no babymama drama."

"I can say the same thing about you, but I ain't worried about your baby daddy. So, don't worry about my BM."

"Oh, trust and believe I'm not worried."

"Good." He winked. "You going with me after this." Dazzle didn't reply. All she could do was smile. It felt good to be desired by a nigga with money. He was certainly an upgrade from Tron's trifling ass.

"Now that y'all got that out the way, can we get to work now?" Kilo teased.

"Oh, you wanna be the only nigga with a chick in the trap house? Cool, bro," he joked.

"Nah." Kilo held his hands up. "Do ya thang, shit. Sis grown."

"Well, we do have work to do. So let's get to it." Tori grabbed a pair of latex gloves from the box and put them on.

"Where's the bathroom?" Dazzle asked.

"Down the hall and to the right." Tori replied. "Hurry up, so I can show y'all how to bag up the work for the corner boys."

Tori used a pocket knife to poke a hole in a key of coke. Carefully, she dumped some onto the scale. Her eyes landed on Lala. "This is how much it needs to say whenever you bagging up an eighth," she pointed at the digits on the scale.

"Okay." Lala nodded her head.

"Goddamn!" Fresh shouted.

"What?" Tori screeched. When she looked up at Fresh, his eyes were not on her. That made her curious as to what he was looking at. Following his eyes, they landed onto Dazzle's half-naked body. She was standing there in her bra and panties. "Girl, what are you doing?"

Dazzle looked down at her smooth, brown skin and shrugged her shoulders. "What?"

"Where are your clothes?" Tori asked.

"In the living room. I saw *New Jack City*, isn't this how I'm supposed to be?"

Kilo and Fresh busted out into a fit of laughter. "Sis, you wild as fuck. Put your damn clothes on."

Fresh interrupted quickly. "She can leave them bitches off."

"Yeah, I bet," Lala added.

"I'll be back." Dazzle walked off and Fresh was heavy on her trail.

For the next few hours, they spent their time bagging up ounces and eighths for the corner boys, while leaving the keys for the big boys. That equaled out to five bricks. The remaining twenty bricks were to be sold for eighteen bands a piece, which was cheaper than the going rate of twenty-two. All they had to do was spread the word.

Tori still had control over her original crew, so that was the easy part. With a new mission at hand, Kilo and Tori paid their crews a visit to get them ready for the shipment when Lala, Dazzle and Fresh left the house. Their last stop was to the corner store in the city. Kilo brought the car to a complete stop and put it in park.

"Last stop. Make it happen."

"I got this," she assured him.

"Let me know if you need reinforcement."

"Trust me, it won't be a problem. He know what time it is."

"He better if he know what's best for his ass." Kilo was ready to lay down anybody at any given moment.

Tori opened the door and stepped out like the boss bitch she was. The clacking sound of her heels grabbed her worker's attention. As usual, he was on the corner getting to the money and gambling. Jarvis picked up the dice and shook them. In his peripheral vision, he spotted Kilo leaning against the hood of his car.

"Boss Lady, what a pleasant surprise."

Marcus leaned up against the wall. "Damn, beautiful." He was damn near drooling, but Tori ignored his comment.

"Hey, Jarvis. What's up?"

"Shit, you know me. Just hustling and beating this nigga ass in dice. Wassup?"

"I need to talk to you in private." Her eyes cut in Marcus' direction. When he didn't get the hint, Jarvis spoke up.

"Step off, bro. Let me holla at her real quick." Marcus stepped away and went inside the store. "What's good?"

"I have the re-up we need to get things back on track. From now on, I won't be working for my father. I have a new connect. That means, don't step on his soldier's toes. The last thing I need is problems."

Jarvis' ears perked up. "Word?" He stroked his chin. "What, y'all beefing or some shit?"

"No. It's nothing like that. I'm building my own empire and the last thing I need is to be beefing over Diesel's territory. For the record, this stays between us. I just want to start fresh and keep a low profile." Placing her hand on her hip, she looked him in the eyes. "Can you handle that?"

"Yeah. I got you, Boss Lady." He held his right hand up in the air like a witness on the stand. "The only beef I want is steak."

"Good. Tomorrow, I'm going to send you the location to grab your re-up."

"I'll be waiting, 'cause I'm out of product. My ass was about to hit up your pops if you didn't come through."

"Everything is back to normal. No more interruptions."

"I hope not, 'cause a nigga gotta eat and so do my seeds."

"Just be ready when I call." Tori turned away from Jarvis and went back to the car.

Chapter 7

Tori stood at the end of the table in a pair of black leather pants, a see-through silk top and a pair of red bottoms on her feet. Her long, jet black hair hung to the arch in her back. Kilo stood by her side as the enforcer. He was ready to knock a nigga noodles loose.

Kilo wore a nasty mug on his face, as he eyed every soldier present. "A'ight, y'all niggas know why this meeting being held, but I'm not gone speak on it. I'm a let the queen handle this business." He kissed her on the cheek. "You got the floor, baby."

"Thank you, baby," she smiled. Then she turned her attention to their workers.

"Last week, work was distributed to all of you and so far, we've only seen forty thousand dollars. I have a problem with that. We still have keys of coke just sitting here, 'cause the shit ain't going nowhere. Anybody care to explain what the fuck going on? And not everybody answer at once." Tori folded her arms under her breast.

The first person to speak up was Jarvis. "I'm a keep it a hunnid with you. It's hard to push this shit when Diesel out here running shit. He got Palm Beach and Broward on lock. This shit ain't like it was when you was working for him. These niggas scared to switch sides."

"It sounds like you scared of him. When in reality, you need to be scared of me. And furthermore, what the fuck happened to your clientele? You mean to tell me they not buying work from you? The supplier doesn't matter, so miss me with that bullshit."

The young corner boy who hustled with Jarvis sucked his teeth and mumbled slick remarks under his breath. Tori didn't hear him, but Kilo did. He stepped forward with his hands folded.

"What was that lil' nigga?" he spat.

The boy was startled. "Huh?"

"You heard what the fuck I said. Now repeat yourself." Kilo was fuming. A small vein popped out on the side of his forehead as he gritted his teeth.

"I-I didn't say nothing," the boy stuttered with wide eyes.

"Yes the fuck you did. Now repeat it." Kilo drew his gold Desert Eagle and aimed it at the frightened teen. "Don't make me repeat myself."

The teen was nervous and he lost control of his bodily functions as he pissed in his pants. "I said... I said that she should go out and try to sell this shit and see how hard it is."

"Nigga, we run this shit. That's what the fuck we pay you for. But, I see you need to be taught a lesson."

"No. Please," he pleaded.

Kilo shifted his eyes towards Tori. "I think you need to school this nigga." Then he passed her the gun.

Tori didn't waste any time taking the heat from his hand and aiming it at his target. *Boc!* The bullet released in what felt like slow motion and slammed against the center of his skull. Blood splatter painted the wall behind him. Jarvis was in shock as the bright red fluid splashed onto him. The reality quickly set in that Tori had just murdered his close friend.

"What the fuck?" Jarvis used his shirt to clean his face.

"Is there a problem?" Kilo needed to be clear if he needed to set another example.

Jarvis quickly spoke up. He didn't want any trouble. "Not at all, fam. I'm cool," he lied. Full of fear, he sat quietly. His only goal was to leave out the same way he came in, without a body bag.

"Do anybody else have a problem before we continue?" The room nodded, signaling that there was no problem. "Let this be a teachable moment for all of you. Don't ever disrespect my wife again. Or you will meet the same fate as this fool."

Kilo's authority turned her on. In fact she could feel the juices stirring between her legs. Turning her attention back to the group, she grinned. "Don't let this pretty face fool you. I will kill you without breaking a nail or batting a lash."

Tori sat down at the table and continued with the meeting like there wasn't a bloody corpse slumped at the table. "Now, where was I?" She snapped her finger, trying to remember. "Oh yeah. Going forward, we need to handle this problem with my father.

He's standing in my way and I can't have that. I've tried to talk to him, but he's not listening."

Fresh listened attentively, then leaned forward. "So, what's the plan? I got money to make and I don't need nobody standing in my way."

"The plan is to take over Broward County. He can keep Palm Beach. So we need to focus on getting a handle on Deerfield, Pompano and Fort Lauderdale. Handle anybody that's trying to ride with us, but be discreet. The last thing we need is to start a beef over turf. Anybody can get it, except my father. Do not touch him, period."

"Ion know, T." Fresh shook his head. "You sure you wanna go up against your blood like that?" He needed to be sure he heard her correctly.

"Yep. He claims I'll never make it in the drug game because I'm a female. But I'm about to show him."

"Say no more. I'm down," Fresh agreed.

The meeting continued for another twenty minutes before it came to an end. Kilo pointed at Jarvis. "Aye, clean up your homie's mess and make sure that muthafucka squeaky clean."

Jarvis didn't utter a single word. Instead, he hopped right up and sprang into action. One hour later, the area was fully scrubbed and the body had been wrapped to discard at an undisclosed location. Finally Jarvis was able to leave, but the guilt of being unable to save his friend ate at him.

Once the house was clear, the couple retired to the bedroom for the remainder of the afternoon. Kilo sat down on the bed, while Tori stood between his legs. Admiring her curves, he caressed her hips and made his way to her soft cheeks.

"Damn, you fine with this on. Boss shit!" He licked his lips, while placing his thumb on hers. That was her signal to lean forward and kiss him. After a slight tongue kiss, he looked into her brown eyes. "I love the way you handled business. The key to being respected in these streets is to make niggas fear you. They need to know you won't hesitate to pull that trigger. When someone disrespects you, make sure you set that example right then and there. Never let anyone slide. The moment you do that is the moment you lose all respect. They'll feel like they can try you."

Nodding her head, she agreed.

"So, what's your plan? How do you plan on handling your father? You need to be very cautious and serious if you gone do that. It needs to be calculated."

Tori placed her hands on his shoulders. "I'm thinking as we speak. Are you having doubts?"

"You know I'm 'bout whatever. I don't fear not one nigga walking the planet, so I'm riding with you on whatever you choose. My loyalty belongs to you," he assured his woman.

Grabbing his handsome face, she pecked his lips. Kilo had grown to be a fine man. His prison stint enforced a mean workout and increased the artwork on his body. He was certainly tatted up like a subway in Harlem, from his neck to his legs.

"My loyalty belongs to you too. I'll kill anybody to protect you, because I know you'll do it for me with no hesitation."

"You better know that shit." Grabbing her waist, he pulled her down onto his lap. "What are you thinking?" he pried.

"I'm going to make sure they can only buy from us."

"How do you plan on doing that?"

"I'm going to hit his stash houses and take all of his work. They'll need more and I'll be the only one with it."

"Okay, so when you want to do this?"

"Tomorrow."

"Okay. I'll round up my boys."

"No. I don't want you involved with this."

"What you mean you don't want me involved?" Kilo didn't like the idea of her going without him. But there was one thing he knew about Tori. Once she had an idea in her head, there was no changing her mind.

"I can slip in and get it with no problem. I'm not trying to start a war, because you know it'll come back to your dad. Just please let me handle this on my own. I promise I know what I'm doing."

"I'll let you do it alone, but I need to be close by in case something goes wrong. That's your only option." He had to put his foot down one way or another. Tori agreed.

***

The next night

The streets were dark and quiet. There wasn't a single human being in sight. A perfect time to commit a crime. That was exactly what Tori expected when she pulled up outside of the meat packing warehouse where Diesel kept his drugs.

"There is one security guard sitting inside the office. He has cameras in here, but there are a few blind spots. Make sure you follow me closely. As soon as we get inside, we have to disable the cameras. He tends to watch from home at times."

"Got it," Dazzle and Lala replied, while putting on their ski masks and putting a bullet in the chamber of their Glock forties.

Tori killed the engine on the minivan she rented and slipped on her ski mask as well. Then she grabbed the sledgehammer from the passenger side and tucked Kilo's Desert Eagle in her waist. "Let's go."

All three women emerged from the van wearing baggy men's clothing to throw them off their trail. Tori looked behind her at the car that sat a few feet away. It was Kilo and Fresh on standby, just in case something popped off. Discreetly, the girls moved towards the back of the building, carrying two large suitcases. The door was secured with a padlock.

"Back up," Tori instructed them.

"That's going to be too loud, don't you think?" Lala asked.

"Yeah, but this is the best way to enter. We need to catch him from behind. Just be ready to shoot if necessary."

Using the sledgehammer, Tori swung it. The lock moved, but it didn't break. Applying a little more muscle, she swung it harder and the lock broke with no problem. Dropping the hammer, she pulled the door open so they could enter.

They snuck down a dimly lit hallway like thieves in the night, with their guns clutched in their hands. Once they made it to the glass room, Tori leaned against the wall and peeked inside. She could see the security guard was occupied, based on the rapid movement of his right hand. His head leaned against the rear of the seat and his eyes were shut.

Tori slowly turned the knob and pushed the door open. The sound of his grunts confirmed what she already knew. Discreetly she crept up behind him and slammed the butt of the gun against his skull.

"Argh! What the fuck?" he shouted, while holding the gash on his head, as the blood flowed heavily.

The woman who was on her knees let out a loud scream. "Ahh!"

"Shut the fuck up!" Lala hit her in the face with a closed fist.

Tori stood in front of him and raised his head. "This why you can't do your job 'cause you trying to get some pussy?"

"What do you want? Please don't kill me. I have a wife and kids."

She ignored his pleas. "Pass me some zip ties." Dazzle reached inside her pocket and passed them to her. "Tie that bitch up," she demanded.

Tori then stood behind him and kicked the chair. The security guard hit the floor with a loud thud. Then she walked over to the computer and disabled the cameras. "If you want to live, I advise you to sit in here until we leave. And when Diesel asks you who did this, tell him some men came in and held you at gunpoint, got it?"

"I got it." He nodded his head rapidly. "I won't tell him, I promise."

"I know you won't. Because if you do, I will make you watch me kill your wife and kids before I kill you." Tori reached inside his pocket and took his wallet. Rumbling inside, she pulled out his driver's license. Jerome Smith, I know where you live. Now, what are you going to tell him?" Dazzle and Lala just stood back and watched their sister from another mister in action.

"Six niggas ran in here with guns and caught me off guard when I came out the bathroom."

"Good." Before they left the office, Tori grabbed the keys and locked the door behind them. Then she called Kilo to join them so they could clean house. Twenty minutes later, the warehouse was empty and they were on their way back home.

Twelve hours later

Diesel was furious after receiving a call that his meat packing warehouse had been hit for all of his work. He was ready to go to war with whomever was bold enough to pull such a stunt. Stepping from the truck, he walked inside the building. As usual, he was dressed to the nines in a Versace silk shirt, slacks and the matching gold and black loafers.

In the packing room, his goons had the security guard and his bitch tied up to a chair with gags in their mouths. He walked up and snatched the rag out his mouth. "What the fuck happened?"

Jerome could hear Tori's voice in his head and the threat he was sure she would make good on. "I was in the bathroom and when I came out, I was confronted by three dudes wearing all-black and ski masks. The one calling the shots hit me in the head and tied me up."

Diesel wasn't buying that bullshit for one second. "Ski masks, huh? That's convenient."

"I'm telling the truth, I swear."

His attention then went to the woman dressed in a skimpy dress with runny Halloween makeup. There was so much fear in her eyes. "Why the fuck is she in here?"

"Um. She. Um—"

Before he could say another word, Byrd jumped in. "This nigga was in here getting some pussy. That's why he couldn't see nobody coming in here. All these state of the art cameras, nigga, and you didn't see nobody coming in here?"

"Is that true? You was in here fucking when you were supposed to be watching my shit?" Several veins appeared on the side of his neck as he gritted his teeth.

Jerome was busted. There was no way out but the truth, so he had to save his own ass. "Yes, but it was dark. It was hard to see any movement and they came in through the back door."

"I wouldn't give a fuck if they came through the ceiling like muthafuckin' ninjas. You were supposed to kill them bitches. Nigga, you ex-military. What the fuck you think I hired you for?"

"I'm sorry."

"Sorry not gone replace my dope or money." Diesel pulled a chrome Colt .45 and placed his finger on the trigger. Snatching the gag from the female's mouth, he tossed it onto the floor. "How many times have you been here?"

In an effort to save her life, she told the truth. "A lot. He always calls me to come keep him company and to have sex."

Diesel's eyes looked like eight balls on a pool table. "See, nobody knows about this place, except for the people who are present. To me, it sounds like you probably stole my shit, or this bitch set you up. Who knows you here?" he asked the frightened woman.

"No one. I swear," her voice trembled.

"You sure about that?"

"I'm positive," she nervously stated, unaware of her fate.

"I believe you." Diesel aimed the gun at her and pulled the trigger twice.

Boc! Boc! Her head popped like a melon.

"Did anybody check the footage?" Diesel spoke in general, but his eyes were on Byrd.

"He said they turned them off."

Diesel handed his gun to Byrd, while he removed his shirt and passed that on as well. "I'm going to ask you one more time who stole my shit. And you better produce me an answer."

"Diesel...come on, man, you don't have to do this. I've been knowing you for years and I've never stolen anything from you. My family needs me."

72

"Do you know that the majority of the people who will cross you first in life are your own family members, friends and people that you've helped?"

"I'm not responsible for this."

Diesel grabbed the gun from Byrd and placed the barrel under Jerome's chin. "And I'm not responsible for this. I'll make sure your wife gets your last paycheck." He fired one shot, then placed three slugs to his chest for good measure. When his work was done, he tucked his gun away and put on his shirt. "Clean this shit up."

His flunkies scrambled to clean up the mess. Byrd stood there with his hands at his side. "What you need me to do?"

"Take his wife five thousand dollars and let her know I'll pay for his funeral arrangements."

"Okay."

"I'm going home to watch this footage. Make sure the place is spotless before they leave here. Then call a cleaning surface to come in and clean it again." Diesel had murder on his mind. He was about to put out a bounty on whoever was responsible and he wanted them dead or alive.

Chapter 8
One month later

On one side of town, business was booming for Tori and Kilo. The quality and price of their work spread in the streets faster than a STD in a prostitution ring. The couple managed to rake in two million dollars easily, since Kilo put down on several crews and took Diesel's stash. His motto was simple, they either got down with the crew or laid down in their final resting place. They had multiple neighborhoods on lock and regular distributors copping work at a wholesale price.

Now on the opposite side of town, the drug business wasn't doing so well. In fact, his operation was suffering. The hit at the warehouse put a damper on things and now he was catching grief from his supplier about having a clean pipeline.

Diesel paced the floor with his hands in his pockets. "Can anybody tell me why in the fuck my weight ain't selling? What the fuck is going on? And who the fuck selling dope on my turf?"

His voice boomed through everyone's eardrums, but they didn't utter a single word. Their silence infuriated him even more. "You motherfuckers better speak up, before I paint my walls with your blood and brain matter." Diesel grabbed his fully-loaded pistol from the table.

Sherrod saw the seriousness in his eyes and spoke up immediately. "I don't know shit, but I can tell you who does."

"Fuck you waiting on? Spill it," he barked.

"That nigga, Jarvis. He said he has a new connect and he getting his work at a cheaper price than yours."

"Who the fuck is it?"

"I don't know. He wouldn't tell me." Sherrod paused for a second. "All I know is that he been talking to your daughter. I saw them talking at the corner store in the city."

Diesel finally stopped pacing the floor and stared him dead in the eyes. "When? What were they talking about?"

"It was a while ago. I didn't hear the conversation cause I was on the inside, but she was there with her nigga, Kilo."

"Kilo!" Diesel frowned. Against his better judgment, he knew she wouldn't leave him alone. "Why are you just now telling me this?"

"Honestly, I didn't think nothing of it. They both work for you, so I figured it was related to that." Sherrod stretched and scratched his head. "You know me, I'm just trying to stay out the way. If it ain't affecting my pay, I don't let it affect my day."

Diesel gritted his teeth and a mean scowl appeared on his face. "Nigga, what fuckin' meeting you attending? I just said shit coming up short, 'cause y'all not getting rid of this dope. Fuck you listening to?"

"I'm eating. I don't know about the rest of these niggas," he boasted arrogantly.

Diesel pulled out his chair and sat down, while pointing his finger in Sherrod's direction. "I want you to bring Jarvis to me. This nigga got some explaining to do. I cut off Tori's dope supply a month ago." Suddenly, he froze and his mind got to wondering. The last thing he wanted to think of was his daughter being responsible for the hit at the warehouse. It was possible. She was smart enough to pull it off and the only person that would try him.

"So, what you want me to tell him?" Sherrod asked.

"Tell that nigga to come see me now!" he shouted, as he pounded his fist on the table.

"A'ight." Sherrod sat back and folded his arms across his chest.

Diesel frowned. "Nigga, why you still here? Go get that nigga, now."

Without another word, Sherrod got up and left the kitchen. The rest of the crew was sitting at the table with blank expressions on their faces. "The rest of y'all niggas can go outside until Sherrod gets back."

One of his soldiers spoke up. "Yo, D, it's hot outside. You trippin' bro."

"You heard what the fuck I said. Now take yo' ass outside and sit up under a tree or some shit."

Once the room was empty, Byrd sat across from his day-one. Before he spoke, he cleared his throat. "I'm telling you now, Tori pushing weight."

"But how? She didn't have any work left. Well, at least to my knowledge."

"Tori is a natural born hustler, D. You raised her. No matter how much you try to deny it, she's just like you."

"So, what you trying to say?"

Byrd hesitated before he laid it on the line. "Tori's not going to stop. That means she's going to interfere with our business. These thirsty ass niggas gone work with her, just so they can get close. I'm telling you right now, you gone have to put an end to what she doing."

Diesel listened attentively, as the wheels in his head turned. As he cracked his knuckles, he nodded his head. "Oh, I'm definitely shutting shit down if I find out Tori going against the grain. But then again, she doesn't have a connection to the streets like I do."

Byrd looked at Diesel like he had two heads. "Nigga, have you met your daughter?"

"We'll see about that." Diesel smirked.

"Let me ask you a question, D. Tori is my niece and I love her to death, but has it ever crossed your mind that she might be behind the hit, bro?" Byrd peeped the blank expression on his face, as if he were having thoughts of his own. "Hear me out. Who has the most to gain from taking you down? Who's bold enough to do it? Who all knew about the meat packing warehouse?"

Byrd gave him more to think about, but it wasn't nothing that he hadn't thought of. All he did was add fuel to the fire. "I've been thinking about that, but I don't want to believe that she'd do that to me."

"Just think about it. Not one person has spoken on this incident since it went down. You know niggas would've been bragging about hitting your shit." Byrd really had the wheels in his head turning.

One hour later

Diesel was sitting at the table, puffing on a Cohiba, when Sherrod walked in with Jarvis trailing behind him. The two men took a seat, then looked over at Diesel. "Heard I was summoned."

"You heard right." Diesel placed his cigar in the ashtray and leaned back in his seat. "I heard you have some valuable information for me."

Unbeknownst to Diesel, Sherrod had already put Jarvis up on game. Therefore, he was aware of the line of questioning heading in his direction. "And what would that be?"

"Word on the street is that you still in business with my daughter. Is that correct?"

Jarvis thought about the conversation he had with Tori about being discreet. Then he glanced at Diesel, who wore a devilish mean mug on his face. That was the moment he decided it was in his best interest to keep it one hundred. Just as he formulated his sentence, Diesel was on his trail heavily.

"Be careful with the lie that's about to roll off your tongue," he gritted his teeth.

"I wasn't about to lie." Sherrod exhaled and sang like a bird.

Chapter 9

"So what happened to you yesterday?" Tori walked inside Tweety's apartment and looked around. "You said you were coming, but you didn't show up."

Tweety rolled her eyes before locking the door and turning to face her best friend. The last thing she wanted as a grown ass woman, was to be questioned. "Honestly, I don't want any parts of that. Selling dope is a deadly game." She shrugged her shoulders. "I just don't want any parts of that. I'm too cute to go to prison, Tori."

Tori sat on the sofa and crossed her legs. "Well, I appreciate your honesty. That's all you had to say the first time. You didn't have to lie about it."

"Technically, it wasn't a lie. I was in deep thought, so I slept on it. When I got up the next morning, I changed my mind."

Tori couldn't believe her ears. The comment actually blew her. It caused her to sit up in her seat. "In other words, you don't want to

get this money? You're comfortable working a minimum wage job, working paycheck to paycheck and barely making it?"

Tweety sighed heavily. One thing she knew, saying no to Tori was like spitting on her face. "This life is not for me. I'm not built like you, Tori. You've wanted to be like your dad for as long as I could remember." Her eyes fell to the floor. "I'm sorry if I offended you, but I'm going to pass on the offer. Please understand that."

Tori stood up and clutched her purse. "You right about one thing. You're not built like me. I'm about the hustle. I refuse to live hand to mouth. That's your thing."

"Please don't judge my life because my idea of success isn't fancy enough in your eyes."

"You got it, sis. No judgment. This was a one-time offer. I have to go."

Tori walked out the door and slammed it behind her. Making a dash to her car, she jumped in and peeled out as quickly as she came. The stereo was bumping loud and hard, as she floated on I-95 doing eighty miles an hour. Thoughts of being on top made her smile as she bumped "Empire State of Mind" by Jay Z. The plan was to take over Broward County slowly, then expand. Diesel would have no choice, but to respect her get-down.

Suddenly, the music stopped and her ringtone flooded through the speakers. Tori frowned and huffed. "Think about the devil and they call." Against her better judgment, she answered anyway.

"Yes?"

"Don't sound so happy to hear from me. You're still my daughter and I love you. I just want the best for you. Not this street shit."

It was understandable for him to feel that way, but that didn't give him the right to try and control her life. "I love you too, but I don't understand why you won't just let me live my life as I see fit."

"Tori, it's obvious you don't know what's best for you. The dope game is treacherous. Your enemies could be men and women. This is not what I had planned for you."

"Since when? The last time I checked, you allowed me to work for you after graduation."

Diesel was getting frustrated. He massaged his temple and tried his best to remain calm. If he was too aggressive his plan would fail and that wasn't the goal. "Listen to me, baby. I only did that because I wanted you to see firsthand how dirty the game can be. Instead of it deterring you in the right direction, it backfired and now you're stuck living this not-so glamorous life."

"This life afforded me a lot growing up and it's the life I'm choosing. I'm sorry you don't agree with that."

"Tori, you only saw the glamorous parts of it. It was my job to keep the bad underneath the radar. You have no idea what you'll be getting yourself into."

"I'll be okay. No one is going to do anything to me. You taught me everything I know and if I need to use it, I will."

"Come over. We need to have a face-to-face."

Tori did her best to remain respectful. Torin Price was still her father. "Dad, if you trying to get me over there to talk about college, I'm not coming. My mind is already made up."

Diesel hummed into the phone. "Your mother would kill me if she saw what I allowed you to become. I know she's rolling over in her grave."

The phone went silent. A few sniffles could be heard. Diesel knew he had his daughter just where he wanted her to be. In her feelings and vulnerable.

"I know this is hard for you. Hell, it's still hard for me. Just come over so we can talk and spend some time together. I miss that. Also, I have some items that belonged to your mother I think you would love to have." That was the icing on the cake.

"I'm on my way," she sniffled.

Tori hung up the phone and wiped her tears away. Her mother's death still took a toll on her heart. Bianca was her best friend and she missed her terribly. If heaven had a phone, she would call her mother every single day. Getting off on the Boca Raton exit, Tori headed west to her father's home.

In the driveway, she spotted a brand-new Acura TL with a paper tag. Stepping from her car, she walked pass the vehicle and peeked inside. The first thing she noticed in the back was a car seat and some toys.

The front door swung open, as she stepped up onto the porch. Diesel stood there with a blank expression on his face. Once she was within arm's reach, Diesel reached out and hugged his daughter tight. It was evident she had been crying, based on the dried-up tear streaks on her face.

"I'm sorry for upsetting you. I didn't mean to." Tori sniffled and nodded her head. True enough, she missed her dad, but that didn't change the way she wanted to live her life. There was no changing her mind.

Tori followed behind Diesel, as he made his way into Bianca's old room. To her surprise, everything was already in boxes. She turned to face him with her big doe eyes. "You packed her things already? How could you?"

"Tori, it's been three years. Don't you think it's time for me to move on? I mean, she's gone. Bianca is never coming back and there's nothing I can do about that."

"No!" Tori shouted. "I haven't moved on and you shouldn't either. Have you even grieved properly?" Tori walked over to the dresser and picked up the photo of her and Bianca, when she was five years old. Tears rolled down her brown cheeks. When she looked up, Diesel's eyes were locked with hers.

"That day keeps replaying in my head. It was the worst day of my life." Tori used the back of her hand to wipe her eyes. "Do you know what's crazy?"

"What's that?"

"Ever since Mom died, I've never seen you cry."

"I've had my moments behind closed doors." Diesel stepped closer and placed his hand on her shoulder. "Being strong for you was my only concern. You needed me more than anything."

"Did you even love Mom?"

The line of questioning was hitting him hard in the chest. Granted, he wasn't an emotional person, the thought alone made him weak. His guilt was eating at him, but there was nothing he could do to change the past.

"I did." Diesel wiped the lone tear that escaped his dark, devious eyes. "I loved your mother more than life itself."

"That's funny, because it didn't seem that way." Tori pulled away from him and moved towards the bed Bianca once slept on. As she sat down, she folded her arms across her chest. Tears dripped as she stared at the floor.

"I remember on my sixteenth birthday, you hit her in front of me. You called her out her name and you were very disrespectful towards her. You used to tell me not to allow a man to mistreat me, but I watched you mistreat my mother." Tori looked up with pain in her eyes. "That was the day I hated you."

The venomous words from her lips cut him deep. His heart shattered into a million pieces. To hear his only daughter say she hated him was a different type of pain. Far worse than Bianca's death.

"Do you still feel that way?" Honestly, he was afraid to hear the answer, but he needed to know the truth.

Tori didn't want to hurt his feelings, but it was time to stop holding back the way she felt. "Sometimes I do and sometimes I don't. I just want all of this pain to go away."

"Wow! I didn't know you felt that way."

"I love you because you are my father, but it's obvious to me that you have some underlining issues with me as well. And in order for us to move past this, we need to be one hundred percent honest with each other."

Diesel stroked his beard and leaned up against the dresser. "Well, since you put it that way, I do have a problem that I need to address with you."

"And what would that be?"

"Word on the street is that you're back hustling. Also, you have a team moving weight for you. Is that correct?"

There was no point in lying. Especially, since someone had opened their mouth. This wasn't the way she wanted it to come out, but hey, they were at that moment and there was no turning back. "It's true. I have my own operation now. You didn't want me in your organization, so I started my own thing."

"Tori, why would you do that?"

"You thought I was going to back down because you kicked me out and left me to fend on my own? No. You knew better than to think that. You raised me. What did you expect?"

Diesel felt defeated. His plan ultimately failed. "I expected you to come back and tell me you were ready to go off to college. Not this!"

"Well, you were wrong. This is my life and I'm damn good at what I do."

"Let me guess. Kilo put you up to this?"

Tori was a bit stunned by the information he wielded at her. It was obvious her attempts to stay under the radar failed. "No, but he's helping me. This was my idea."

"You just don't listen. Every attempt I've made to save you has not worked."

Tori rose to her feet. "You thought banning me was going to make me stop? You're wrong."

"What do I have to do to make you stop?" he pleaded.

"There's nothing you can do. I've made my decision. I need for you to accept me for what and who I am."

Diesel leaned up from the dresser. "I don't think you know who you are."

"No. You don't know who I am."

"I know you and your little crew is stepping on my territory. If you knew anything about the game, you'd know that's grounds for termination."

"You're wrong. My crew was advised to stay off your territory and out of the way."

"It's clear someone isn't listening and I advise you to fix it before I do. Get out the game, Tori. This isn't for you."

"Is that a threat?" she asked.

"Take it how you want." Diesel cracked his knuckles. "I'm going to give you one last chance to shut your operation down and go to school. Be better than me."

Tori grabbed the suitcase that housed her mother's items and walked towards the door. Hesitantly, she turned back to face him. "Don't worry, I'm going to better than you. I promise. Just wait on it. I'm going to be the Queen of the Trap."

"Over my dead body."

Tori ignored his last comment and left the room. If Diesel thought he could threaten her into stepping down, he was sadly mistaken. Tori was about to go hard in the paint. By the time the dust settled, she was going to be on top, rocking that crown.

Chapter 10

The sun was beaming hard at ten in the morning. Dazzle casually strolled down the sidewalk and up to her apartment. Little specks of sweat were present on her forehead. Sleep was heavy in her eyes, but that didn't stop her from seeing the bright pink papers stuck to her door.

"What the fuck? I know I don't owe them shit." She groaned, while snatching it off. Due to the fact that she had been late on several occasions, she knew what it was all about. However, it didn't make sense, because she had been paying her rent on time.

Dazzle unlocked the door and stepped inside. The apartment was cold and quiet. That meant Tron and Jamir were still sleeping. Before she thought about crashing for the morning, she opened the letter. Quickly, she read line for line and with each word, her blood boiled and her heart rate increased tremendously. Dazzled clutched the letter tight in her hand and raced for her bedroom door. To her surprise, the room was empty. That was when she rushed to Jamir's room. It was empty too.

"Where the fuck they at?" she mumbled, while high-tailing it back to the living room to retrieve her phone.

Dialing his number, she waited on him to pick up. The phone rang to no avail before she heard the voicemail. Ending the call, she called again. This time he picked up.

"Hello," his voice was low and groggy.

"Where the fuck you at with my baby?"

"Aye, don't call me talking all loud and shit. We at my mama house. What's the problem?"

"You my problem. Why the fuck you at your mama house?"

"Bitch, are you serious?"

"Don't call me out my name. And since you wanna talk shit, why the fuck do I have an eviction note on my motherfucking door? I gave you the money to go and pay it. So, what the fuck you did with my money?"

Tron's eyes widened in surprise. He was hoping to have flipped the money and paid the rent before they sent out the notice. Raising up, he pushed Tweety's head from between his legs. "I fucked up, but I'm going to handle it."

"What the fuck you mean by you fucked up?"

"I used the money to flip it, but I haven't made all the money back yet."

"You better get my shit up and pay my damn rent. Ole stupid ass make me sick. You can't do shit right." Dazzle began to shed tears. "I am so sick of you. Every time I turn around, you have some shit going on."

"Well, stop turning around then, bitch! I said I'm going to get the money up." Tron was fuming. "And you wonder why a nigga act like this. Look at how you talk to me. You a disrespectful ass bitch and I'm sick of you too."

"Pussy ass nigga, I don't give a fuck. If you so sick of me, then get the fuck out my shit. It ain't like you helping me anyway. As a matter of fact, I'll pack your shit up and make it easy for you."

"Good! I'm taking my son too."

"For what? You can't provide for him and you have no place to stay, you bum ass nigga."

"Bum ass nigga? Was I a bum ass nigga when you was choking on my dick? Ho', you hilarious. You think you the world's greatest mother. Meanwhile, you out here shaking your ass for dollars, slutty ass bitch."

It was true that once you made a person mad, they would reveal how they truly felt about you. In the back of her mind she felt it, but now his words confirmed it. The shit stung a bit, but the strip club was about to be a thing of the past.

Dazzle stayed strong and kept her composure. She couldn't reveal how damaged she was, knowing how he truly felt about her. "You know what, Tron, you can't hurt me with your words. I been knew you felt like that and it's cool. Just run me my coins before shit gets bad for you."

"Nothing is worse than being with you. I'll be there to pick up my shit today and don't call me no more. I'm done wit' yo ass."

"I been done with you. Bring my damn son home."

"Fuck you!"

Dazzle heard the line go dead. She was so infuriated with him that she threw her cellphone. Surprisingly, it didn't break. Heartbroken and angry, she retired to her room and laid down. Dazzle knew she wasn't getting that money back, so she pondered on who could help her. After she got some rest, she would try her luck and see how it turned out. What was the worst that could happen? Besides him saying no.

***

Tron sat on the edge of the bed with his head in his hands. It wasn't his intention for things to go that far left, but Dazzle had a way of bringing the devil out of him. Tweety eased behind him and kissed the back of his neck. She was ready for another round, despite him having a huge blow-up with her best friend. Tron was too pissed to entertain her, so he pushed her away.

"Stop!"

"Don't let her upset you. Let me make you feel better." Tweety placed her hands on his stiff shoulders and massaged away.

"How can I not be upset? You heard what just happened. Now I have to find a place to live and going to my old girl house ain't an option."

Tweety and Tron had been sleeping together for three months. Each and every Monday, they linked up to have sex. That was the reason she was never reachable for her girls.

"You can stay here with me. I don't mind." She nibbled on his ear.

Tron closed his eyes and huffed. "That'll never work."

"Yes, it will. They won't suspect a thing. As far as they're concerned, they think I hate your guts."

"You sure about that?"

"Yeah. I did that so they wouldn't be suspicious of us being missing on Mondays."

"We can try it and see what happens, but you need to be sure about this."

Tweety climbed onto his lap and kissed him on the neck. "Of course, I'm sure. It's about time I have some in-house dick. I'm tired of the restrictions. That once a week shit ain't hitting on nothing. I need a dose of you daily."

Tron placed his hands on her soft backside and leaned back onto the bed. "Show me what I'll be getting every day."

Tweety smiled and grinded her naked body on his lap. "Oh, don't you worry. I'm gone always handle business."

"I hope so." He grinned, as he felt his rod slip into that wet-wet.

Four hours later

Dazzle was up and energized. That power nap and shower was exactly what she needed. Now it was time to put her plan in effect. The argument she had with Tron earlier was the furthest thing from her mind and all she wanted to focus on was getting up her rent money. Tori was an option, but she needed to stand on her own two feet. Even if that meant giving up some pussy.

University Drive was thicker than usual, but that didn't deter her from the mission. Nor did it take long for her to pull up in the secluded complex. Before Dazzle got out the car, she sprayed herself with some Victoria Secret's body spray. The sun eased up a bit and the wind was now blowing.

The complex was extremely quiet and she could see why he chose the spot in the first place. Stepping from the elevator, she walked up to apartment 407 and tapped lightly on it. When the door swung open, she smiled.

"I'm surprised you showed up. It must be a nigga lucky day." Fresh stepped back and let her inside.

"Must be," she smirked. Dazzle sat down on the sofa and got comfortable.

Fresh sat down beside her and placed his hand on her thigh. His eyes was low and the smell of the weed told her he was higher than a kite. "So, what strong wind blew you my way?"

"I told you I needed help."

"Oh yeah, you did say that. I thought you was bullshitting."

"Nah. I'm dead ass serious."

"Well, come in the room and tell me all about it." Fresh grabbed her hand and escorted her to the bedroom.

Dazzle sat down on the bed with her hands in her lap. The way she fidgeted told him she was nervous. Fresh grabbed the blunt from the ashtray and lit it. He took two long pulls, then passed it to her.

"Loosen up. I'm not going to do anything you don't want me to do." Fresh grabbed the half-drunk bottle of Hennessy from the nightstand and passed it to her. "Sip that."

Dazzle removed the top and drank straight from the bottle. The liquid was hot as hell going down her throat, but that was nothing new for her. In the club, she drank hot liquor quite often. Fresh grabbed the remote and turned the volume up on the television set. The sound of "Facedown" by Brisco flowed through the sound bar. It was no coincidence he played a song about sex and hitting it from the back. That didn't bother her at all. In fact, it turned her on and she anticipated doing just that.

Once the potent drug and alcohol had her comfortable, she removed her shoes and leaned against the headboard. Fresh looked down at her manicured feet and took one into the palm of his hand.

"You have pretty toes."

"Thank you." He definitely had her blushing.

"So, what's up? Tell me what's going on with you."

While Fresh massaged her feet, she told him everything about her relationship with Tron, including the rent money. Reliving that heated argument made her emotional. As much as she tried to fight it, the tears wouldn't stay at bay. Dazzle didn't want to seem weak, but she was vulnerable and couldn't contain her emotions.

Fresh was disgusted at the way Tron disrespected the mother of his child and fucked up her money. In his eyes, that was a pussy move. "Why you fucking with that young ass nigga anyway? It's obvious he don't give a fuck about your well-being or the welfare of his son. As much as me and my BM beef, I'll never drag her through the mud like that. I don't know who raised these pussy ass niggas."

Dazzle shrugged her shoulders. "He wasn't like that in the beginning. He used to take care of me, but then it all changed."

Fresh shook his head. "Nah. That nigga been like that. You just didn't see it."

"You right," she agreed.

"So, what you need me to do? Beat his ass?"

"I only had three days to pay it and I won't have it. Can you loan me the money until I make it back on Saturday?"

Fresh stared into her eyes. "See if you would've gave me some play, you wouldn't be going through this fuck shit right now. The way you brushed a nigga off, I thought he was taking care of home."

Dazzle knew he was right, but her self-esteem was too low for her to see it. She hung her head low. "To be honest, I didn't think you were interested in me like that."

"Humph! You thought I just wanted to fuck?"

"Yeah."

"If I just wanted to fuck, don't you think I would've been paid to smash that ass?"

Dazzle looked at him sideways. "So, what you telling me is that you don't wanna fuck me?"

"Nah. I never said that." He chuckled. "I definitely want some pussy, but that's not all I want." Fresh moved closer to her and placed his hand on the side of her neck. "I wanna change your life."

"How you..." Dazzle's words got caught in her throat when she felt his hand glide up her smooth thigh. His fingers caressed her middle. "How do you plan on doing that?"

"I'll show you. How much money do you need?" he asked while breathing heavily in her ear.

"Sixteen hundred dollars." Dazzle's rent was only eleven hundred dollars. However, her car note and insurance was late and she didn't have all of the money to satisfy the bill.

Fresh paused for a few seconds. When he leaned back and looked into her sad eyes, his heart wanted to help her. But his mind wasn't on the same accord. Against his better judgment, he agreed.

"Listen to me. I like you and I'm willing to help, but don't try to play me."

"I'm not. I promise."

"I'll help you under one condition."

Dazzle was almost afraid to hear what he had to say, but she didn't have any other options. "Okay."

"If I give you this money, you gotta put that nigga ass out." Fresh's facial expression was soft, but his tone was hard and stern. Dazzle knew he meant every word.

"I will."

"No." He shook his head. "I mean today. That nigga cannot sleep there tonight and I mean that shit."

That wasn't a problem. Tron's ass was out the door anyway. All she had to do was clear his shit out of her apartment. "I promise. Me and Tron are history. It's all about me and you now." Dazzle leaned forward and kissed Fresh in the mouth. To seal the deal, she stood up in front of him and removed her clothes. It was time to move on with someone she didn't have to beg or plead with to get money.

Chapter 11
Two days later

Dazzle tossed Tron's remaining clothes and shoes into a trash bag without hesitation. After a successful arrangement with Fresh, she was able to pay her rent, car note and insurance. All she could do at that point was keep her word. Especially, since he broke her off with two thousand dollars. That didn't come easy because in exchange, he tore a new lining in her pussy for that cash. It was worth it though.

On the flipside, she didn't have to pay it back. All she had to do was maintain her status as his girl and he had her back one hundred percent. Dazzle was cool with that. Tossing the bag against the floor, she leaned against the wall.

"Whew! I'm so glad this is over with."

"Me too. I been told you to leave his sorry ass alone. All that nigga did was bring you down." Tweety grabbed the bag and pulled it to the front door. "Now you can move on with your life."

"I know." Dazzle had no plans on revealing her new man just yet. In due time, she would inform her girls, but that was after things looked more promising in their relationship. "It's been a long time coming. Right now I just want to focus on myself and my son."

"Jamir is your main priority, so just focus on him and everything else will fall into place."

"I know." Dazzle reached out and hugged her girl. "Thanks, Tweety for coming over to help me. This was hard, but necessary."

"That's what friends are for." Tweety flashed a bright, devious smile.

The doorbell rang and Dazzle's head swiveled in the direction of the door. Being that she already knew who stood on the opposite side, she opened the door without checking the peephole. "Hey."

"Hey, girl. How are you?"

"I'm good. I can't complain. How about you?"

"Relieved," she sighed. "It's finally over."

"Good. It was well-needed." Tori looked at Tweety with a disappointing stare. "Tweety."

"Hey, Tori."

"I'm about to head out. Dazzle, I'll talk to you later."

"Okay. Thanks again."

"No problem." Tweety grabbed the last bag and walked outside.

Tori couldn't wait to nosedive into what was happening. "Why she leaving here with bags?"

Dazzle took a seat on the sofa and placed her feet underneath her body. "She was over here helping me get rid of Tron stuff."

"Oh, where she taking it to?"

"To Tron."

That caught Tori off guard. "Why? She can't stand him."

"I didn't want to take it to him and I didn't want him over here, so she offered to drop it off to his mama house." Dazzle didn't give a damn who dropped it off, as long as it wasn't her.

"Hmm. I guess." She tooted up her nose.

"Were you going to drop it off for me?"

"Hell no!"

"Thank you. 'Cause I sure as hell wasn't about to do it."

"I just find it odd that she volunteered to do it when she can't stand his ass, but whatever." Tori reached inside her oversized Gucci bag and pulled out a key of cocaine. Placing it on the table, she looked over in Dazzle's direction, who was wearing a blank stare on her face.

"What's that for?"

"Your man. When he come over tonight, give it to him."

Dazzle's left brow dipped low. "What man?"

"Fresh. Don't play crazy."

Dazzle hit her forehead with the palm of her hand. "Oh my gosh! He told you?"

"You didn't."

"Tori, I was going to tell you. It just happened so fast. I mean, I just broke up with Tron and that's bad already."

Tori grabbed her bag and stood up. "Girl, please. Not fast enough. I'm not mad. Fresh is actually a good dude. Just don't do nothing to fuck it up. He'll be good for you and Jamir." Tori stopped and looked around. "Speaking of which, where is he?"

"With Tron."

"Oh. Well, I have to go and finish making my rounds. I'll call you later. Love you, sis."

"I love you too. Be safe."

"Always." Dazzle locked the door and called Fresh.

***

On the way to the corner store in the city, Tori dialed Jarvis' number for the third time. When he didn't answer, she tossed the phone into the passenger seat. "I'm fuckin' his ass up when I catch him."

Ten minutes later, Tori pulled up at the store. The sight of Sherrod and a few of the other soldiers standing out front formed a knot in her stomach. That stunt had Diesel's name all over it. Normally, Kilo would've been with her, but he had other business to handle, so she had to slide solo. Stopping within a few feet of them, she placed her hand on her hip.

"Sherrod, where is Jarvis?"

He grinned and adjusted his fitted cap. "I don't know. I haven't seen him."

"Then why are you standing on his post? You already know who this spot belongs to."

Ever since Diesel threatened her, he had been MIA. No one knew about the issue with her father. Not even Kilo. That was her way of keeping the peace, since it was a family issue. She couldn't have the only men in her life beefing.

"Last time I checked, it belonged to Diesel." Sherrod shoved his hands into his pockets. "But, I don't want no problems, so take it up with your daddy."

Tori wasn't in the mood for his bullshit. She knew exactly who needed to be confronted. As soon as she got in the car, she dialed his number.

"My dearest daughter. What a wonderful surprise. How are you, my dear?"

"What did you do to Jarvis?"

"You cut right to the chase, huh?" Diesel yawned into the phone. "So, you have no conversation for your ole man?"

"Dad, just answer the question please."

"Listen to me, princess. I am trying so hard not to snap right now, but your attitude is making this very difficult for me." Tori rolled her eyes, but she didn't utter a single word. Instead, she listened to what he had to say.

"Now, I've been playing your game for far too long and frankly, I'm sick of it. This is what's going to happen. You're going to bring your ass back home and in the next few days, we are flying out to Atlanta to get you registered for school."

"But, Dad—" she cried.

Diesel wasn't having it. He cut her off immediately. "Be quiet! I am going to pay for your room and board, apartment or whatever it is you want."

"I want my life here."

"Tori, all that queen of the trap is over. Yo' ass getting up out of Florida, whether you like it or not."

Tori waited until his rant was over to prepare him for a rude awakening. "Dad, I love you. I really do, but I'm tired of apologizing for my decision repeatedly. My mind is made up. I'm not going to college and I'm not coming back home. Please respect my decision."

"You're a fucking teenager. You don't know what you want in life. You don't know what's best for you. But I do. Now, for the last time, when are you coming back home?"

Tori's voice was low and shaky. "I'm not."

Diesel stroked his chin. "If you are not home within the next twenty-four hours, everything you have built will crumble at the hands of my soldiers. I will shut down every single spot you are operating from and you'll never sell a key of coke. When I'm finished demolishing your little organization, you won't be able to sell a dime bag of coke in the entire state of Florida."

"We'll see about that." A distraught Tori ended the call and leaned her head against the seat. Their business was in trouble and she didn't know how to tell Kilo. Nor did she know how to fix it.

***

Smoke was pouring from Diesel's ears. With his phone clutched in his hand, he scrolled through his call log and pressed send. The phone rang twice before he got an answer.

"Sherrod?"

"Waddup, boss?"

"Do you have eyes on Tori?"

"Yeah. She up here at the store, but she about to pull off."

Diesel didn't want to resort to his back-up plan, but Tori left him no choice. "I need you to follow her."

"And do what?" Sherrod was curious about the mission.

"Nothing at all. Just observe her." Diesel took a sip of vodka from his glass. "Sherrod!"

"Yeah."

"Don't touch my daughter."

"I'm not, but what you want me to do?"

"Just follow her and see where she's staying. Don't get too close, she's smart. If you see Kilo, bring him to me." Diesel clenched his teeth and grunted. "Do not lay a finger on my baby. If she's with him, don't do anything. Wait until he's alone to make a move and snatch his ass up."

"Got it."

"Don't fuck this up."

"I won't," Sherrod assured him. "I'll be in touch." Shoving the phone into his back pocket, he looked at his boys. "Stay up here and make sure none of them lame ass niggas show up."

"And if they do?" One of the men asked.

"Light they ass up." Sherrod jogged to his black, Dodge Ram truck and fired up the engine. Whipping out, he flushed it down Sistrunk Boulevard, until he spotted Tori's car. Once he was close enough, he trailed her at a safe distance and made sure to stay out of her rearview mirror.

***

Tori arrived at the spot at 5:30 pm. Kilo's car wasn't there, so she was relieved. That gave her enough time to get her shit together. Once inside, she rushed to the bathroom and opened up the pregnancy test she purchased at the nearby Walgreens.

Anxiously, Tori pulled out the stick and sat down on the toilet to administer the home kit. Her fingers trembled as she held the tip. After the stick was saturated with urine, Tori sat it down by her feet and waited on the results. A heavy gush of wind escaped her lips, as she covered her face to catch the light tears. Lately, she had become an emotional mess and she had a feeling she knew the reason. It was the same thing she witnessed Dazzle go through. Not to mention, she had missed her period.

Slowly, Tori removed her hands and looked down at the floor. The sight of two pink lines warmed her heart. To have Kilo's baby was something she always wanted. Both of them for that matter. Ideally, the news of a baby growing inside of her should've been the happiest moment in her life. Instead, it was damn near impossible to celebrate with their business being at stake. Children weren't cheap and they needed money to take care of a family.

From the bathroom, Tori heard the front door slam. In a hurry, she tossed the items in the plastic bag and stuffed the evidence underneath the sink. "Baby, where you at?" Kilo yelled.

Tori cleaned up the mess and washed her hands. "I'm in the bathroom," she yelled, while turning off the light.

Upon her exit into the hallway, she stood face-to-face with the love of her life. Kilo reached out and took her into his arms. Tori stepped into his warm embrace and closed her eyes.

"I missed you while I was gone."

"I missed you too."

The gloominess in her voice made him curious. Gently, he raised her chin and stared into her red eyes. "What's wrong? Why are you crying?"

That was a loaded question that required multiple answers. Therefore, she decided to start with the bad news first. "It's my father."

Kilo knew that was bad news within itself. "What did he do or say now?"

"He threatened to shut down the operation if I don't leave you and go to college." Tori held onto the back of his shirt. "It's so unfair the way he's trying to control my life."

"Come on." Kilo raised her from the floor and into his arms. "Tell me everything that happened."

Kilo laid Tori onto the bed. As she eased to the middle, he followed suit and cuddled up behind her. Kilo listened to the conversation and chain of events that led up to that very moment. In his heart, he sided with his lady. On the other hand, he understood where Diesel was coming from.

"Baby, it's not the end of the world if you go to college."

That was not the response she expected. Tori sat up in the bed and frowned. "You're agreeing with him?"

"No, I'm not. All I'm saying is why risk the lives of our workers by going to war with your father? I don't want to beef with him because I'm going to marry you one day. And eventually we have to come together one day as a blended family."

Tori folded her arms and pouted like a toddler. "I can't believe you. You're supposed to be on my side."

"Baby, I am." He stroked the side of her face. "If this was anyone else, I'd bury that bitch alive, but this is your father we're talking about. I can't kill him. Nor can I make a move against him without putting you in the middle."

Tori sat her emotions to the side and listened to her man. Everything he said was the truth and as much as she wanted to disagree with him, she couldn't.

"Four years is nothing, Tori. By the time you graduate, we'll be in this position. Think about it."

"I did. I don't like it."

"Why not?"

All she could think about was the baby she was carrying. This was their chance to finally build the family that they both want. "You expect me to leave you here for four years? No, I'm not leaving."

Kilo grabbed Tori by the hand. "I'm not going anywhere. I'm not leaving you. I'll be right here waiting on you. And in between time, I'll come and visit. It will work out perfectly."

"No it won't. Our relationship will fail." Tori fought every emotion that threatened to surface. The secret was eating away at her soul and Tori was tempted to tell him the real reason she couldn't leave the state.

"Listen, baby. I'd love for you to stay here with me. Trust me. But at the same time, it's not worth the shit Diesel trying to do."

Tori fell back onto the bed and covered her face. "You just want me to leave so you can cheat in peace. I get it."

"Tori, stop! You know that's not true. I don't want none of these hoes. Those bitches wasn't there when I did my bid. It was you and only you. I owe you the world and I'm going to give it to you."

Tori trusted him without a shadow of a doubt, but it was in her nature to be a brat. "I hear you."

Kilo moved her hand. "What do I need to do to prove to you that I'm not leaving you?" Tori didn't respond. "What, you wanna get married before you leave? We can do that. I'm fine with it."

Tori's eyes lit up, as she looked at his handsome face. "Yes."

"We can go to the courthouse and do it. Then after you graduate, we can have a big ass wedding." Tori agreed.

While the love birds cuddled, sleep fell upon them. The hour hand on the clock moved swiftly and midnight was there within no time. Kilo jumped from his sleep when he heard Tori screaming and crying. When he looked over at her, he realized she was having a nightmare. Without hesitation, he shook her hard.

"Tori! Baby! Wake up, Tori! Open your eyes." Tori's eyes flung open and her face was saturated with tears. Her heart was beating hard inside her chest like subwoofer speakers.

"Are you okay?"

"No," she cried. "I dreamed you were killed and you left me all alone with our baby."

Kilo held her closely to his chest. The strong thump of his heart soothed her soul. Instantly, she was able to catch her breath and relax. "I'll never leave you out here to raise our kids alone. You don't have to worry about that. I'll be right here." In the drug game, going home every night was not promised, but Kilo planned on making that a reality for his future wife.

Chapter 12
Valentine's Day

The following morning, Kilo awakened Tori before the sun lit up the sky. With sleep heavy in her eyes, she yawned and tried her best to focus on what he held in his hand.

"Tori. Can you hear me?"

"Yes, baby. I'm listening."

"I've been up thinking and I don't want to wait any longer."

"What is it, baby?" Tori was trying to make out what he was trying to say.

Kilo popped open a box, revealing a shiny ring. "I want us to go ahead and get married."

Tori jumped up from the bed. The sleep in her eyes had been replaced with pure excitement. "Yes! Yes! When?"

"Today. We can go down to the courthouse."

"What about our friends and family?"

"We can celebrate with them later when I give you your dream wedding. This is our moment. I just want it to be you and me." Kilo slid the ring on her finger.

"Okay. Let's do it." Tori immediately got up and went into the bathroom to get dressed.

Two hours later, Kilo and Tori stood in front of the altar, at the Broward County Courthouse, dressed in all white. Love was definitely in the air. As the pair held hands, they listened attentively as the pastor read a scripture and followed with their vows. Kilo kissed his bride to seal the deal. The service was fast, but Tori was fine with the process. As long as she had her man, that's all that mattered.

On their way down the aisle, Tori observed other couples waiting to get hitched. There was one couple that caught her attention, a pregnant girl. Her stomach was big and round. Tori placed her hand on her own belly as she imagined being that size within the next several months.

Back at the house, Kilo hit Tori with a double dose of loving, since the two wouldn't be taking a honeymoon just yet. Tori rested her head in the crook of her husband's arm, as she traced lines on his firm chest.

"Mrs. Tori Kingsley. I love the sound of that," she giggled.

"I do too," he chuckled. "When I was little, I used to tell my dad I was going to marry you one day."

"Well, you did it."

"We did it."

"All we need now is a honeymoon."

"We can do that. Where do you want to go?"

"Paris."

"Book everything and tell me how much you need."

"Okay." Tori and Kilo closed their eyes and took a nap.

***

By the time Tori got ready to leave the house, Kilo was already in the wind. Money needed to be made and errands had to be run. So, there was no hesitation when it came to him handling business. On the other hand, Tori had a list of things to do, but dealing drugs wasn't one of them. Within the next few weeks, she would be leaving the state to start her new journey. Kilo wouldn't be too far behind. The only thing left to do was prepare for her exit. That included revealing her secret marriage to her friends and telling Kilo about the pregnancy.

Tori set the alarm on the way out and locked the door. The sky was a dark, gloomy gray. That meant the rain wasn't too far behind. Tori decided to go shopping and set the mood for the special night she had planned for Kilo. Since they decided to get married, there was no sense in keeping the pregnancy a secret any longer.

Inside the car, Tori started the engine and put on her seatbelt. Suddenly, she felt the need to be safe. On the way out the driveway, Tori was on cloud nine hundred when she failed to see a black truck coming up the street. Quickly, she slammed on brakes while gripping the steering wheel.

"Shit," she panicked. "Pay attention."

The truck continued to cruise up the street. The tints were extremely dark, which made it difficult to see inside. Tori leaned back in the seat to catch her breath.

***

"Damn, nigga. Slow ya' ass down and steer this motherfucker right. You think I'm trying to die?" Jarvis put on his seatbelt. "You might have a death wish, but I don't. The man said don't touch his daughter." The last thing he needed was trouble with Diesel.

"Shut the fuck up!" Sherrod barked.

"Well, act like it. You damn near smashed the girl's car." The duo had been arguing since they stepped foot in the truck an hour ago.

Sherrod stopped at the stop sign and pulled out a Newport. Jarvis laughed. "Oh, you nervous now," he chuckled. "You pulling the fuck out that cigarette."

Sherrod cracked the window. "Fuck you."

"I would, but I'm tapped out from dropping this log in your sister all night," he joked.

Sherrod cut his eyes in his partner's direction. "Quit playing with me before I bust ya ass."

"Damn, what crawled up your ass?"

"You, nigga. You always fuckin' playing. Now ain't the time. Sit yo' ass in that seat and help me find this nigga." Sherrod's foot hit the gas hard, causing Jarvis to jerk in the passenger seat.

***

The afternoon approached quickly and it was time to settle the beef once and for all. Although, Tori was against the idea, Kilo's reassurance was enough to make her bow down to her father. After leaving the mall, she made her way up to Boca Raton. As usual, the house had a crowd of cars parked out front.

Tori brushed past the workers with an attitude and barged inside the home. On her way up the stairs, her father stopped her.

"What are you doing here, Tori?" He automatically assumed she was there to retrieve her things.

"I came to talk to you."

Diesel leaned against the staircase. "We're beyond the talking stage. If we're not discussing school, there's nothing left to say."

"Actually, that's why I'm here."

"To discuss school?"

"Yes."

The front door opened and Byrd walked inside. "Hey, Tori."

She watched closely as he came in and removed his jacket, revealing a gun tucked in his waistband. "Hey." Her attention went back to her father. "Can we go upstairs and talk in private?"

"Yeah. Come on."

Diesel proceeded up the steps with Tori on his heels. Casually, he moved down the hall and into his bedroom. Once inside, Tori closed the door and sat down on the bed. Nervousness took over her body. It showed by the way her leg shook rapidly. There was an uncomfortable silence between the two, until Diesel decided to break the ice.

"What's going on, Tori?"

Tori rubbed her hands against her jeans to warm her palms. "I just wanted to stop by and tell you I give up. You win."

It was hard to determine his mood because he lacked emotion and he wore the same expressionless face. "How so?"

"I'm out the game. I decided to go to college."

Diesel wasn't impressed. He assumed it was just a ruse to stop him from interfering with her organization. "I don't believe you. Yesterday when we spoke, you were so adamant about staying here and running your operation. Why the sudden change?"

This was her chance to bridge the gap between Kilo and Diesel. Air filled her lungs, then she released it slowly. "Honestly, it was Kilo."

Diesel's eyebrow wrinkled and a huge vein appeared on his forehead. "What did he do to you?" There wasn't a doubt in his mind that the young hustler broke his daughter's heart.

"Last night when I got home, I told him we had an argument about me not going to school." Tori finally looked up to face her father. "Do you know he agreed with you? He said I should leave and to stop being rebellious."

"Hmm," he grunted.

"Despite what you feel about Kilo, he loves me and I love him. He has my best interest at heart and you should appreciate that. Appreciate the fact that he's not cheating on me or abusing me."

Diesel fished around in his pocket for his cellphone, as he listened to his daughter confess her love for a man he despised. Regardless of how he felt about their relationship, he decided to call off the kidnapping. With Tori living in Georgia, Diesel was pretty confident the distance would put a strain on their relationship, and they would call it quits. Besides, there were plenty of boys in Atlanta that would occupy her time.

Suddenly, Tori's phone began to ring from inside her purse. By the ringtone, she knew it was her man calling. Reaching inside, she pulled it out and answered.

"Hey, baby."

"Where you at?"

"In Boca about to leave."

"A'ight. I'm on my way back to the house."

"Okay. I'll meet you there shortly."

"I love you."

"I love you too." Her tone was mushy and a huge smile was plastered across her lips. It made Diesel cringe, but he didn't mumble a word.

Tori stood up. "I have to go, but I love you, Dad." On her way out the door, she planted a soft kiss on his cheek and left.

Diesel rushed downstairs to retrieve his phone from the kitchen counter. To his surprise, he had two missed calls and a text message from Sherrod that read, *I'm about to take off.* In a panic, he called back, but didn't get an answer.

***

Kilo whipped his brand-new silver BMW in the driveway and put the car in park. The buzzing of his cellphone caught his attention, so he dropped his head and grabbed it from the cup holder. It was Tori.

"Yeah, baby."

"Do you want me to grab us some food before I come home?"

"Nah. We going out to dinner with the family, so we can celebrate our marriage."

"Okay. I'll be home in a few minutes."

Kilo froze when he spotted two men approaching his vehicle dressed in all black. "What the fuck?"

"What's wrong, baby?"

Kilo dropped the phone and grabbed the gun that rested on his lap. Sherrod snatched the door open and attempted to unarm his subject. Both men tussled with the weapon. Kilo knew he was out numbered and there was only one way out. Squeezing the trigger, he let off one round.

Boc!

The bullet struck Sherrod in the shoulder, causing him to stumble backwards.

"Kilo!" Tori screamed through the phone, while mashing hard on the gas pedal.

Jarvis stepped in and let off two shots, hitting Kilo once in the chest and in the stomach. "Bro, let's clear it." Jarvis and Sherrod ran back to the truck and fled the scene.

Kilo felt light-headed when he leaned up. Blood coated his fingers when he placed his hand on his chest. "Fuck!"

Sweat protruded from his forehead and he was losing his breath. Using the little bit of strength he had left, he pushed his body forward. On the ground, a wounded Kilo fought for his life, as he struggled to breathe. Images of Tori being pregnant filled his brain. Tears began to roll, as his eyes grew heavier by the second.

"Come on, Tori. Please, baby," he mumbled.

God had to be listening because seconds later, he heard screeching tires, followed by loud screams. Tori had already called the police the second she heard the first shot. Dropping down to her knees, she cradled his head in her lap.

"Help is on the way, baby. Just stay strong. We need you." As she rocked back and forth, she kissed his forehead. "You have to fight, baby. I can't. I can't live without you." Her own tears soaked her face.

"I love you, Tori."

"I love you too." Kilo was fading in and out of consciousness, so she shook him. "No! Don't close your eyes. Don't go to sleep. Please. Stay with me."

"I feel cold, baby." His bottom lip trembled.

"Baby, please don't go. I'm pregnant. I'm having your baby."

A faint smile spread across his lips. "I know. I found your test underneath the sink."

"That means you have to fight."

Kilo was trying his best to stay strong, but the grim reaper was calling his name. "If it's a boy, name him Capone." Just as he uttered his last sentence, they heard sirens.

"Help is on the way." Tori gripped his hand. "You're going to pull through this and we can name him together."

"Keep me close to your heart and take care of our son."

The paramedics rushed towards Tori at a high rate of speed. "I need you to step aside, ma'am. We got it from here."

Tori stood up and watched closely as they made every attempt to save his life.

***

"What the fuck you mean, you shot him?" Diesel yelled. "That's not what I told you to do, you fuckin' idiots."

"He shot Sherrod. What did you expect me to do? Stand around and let him shoot me too?"

"I'll deal with you later. Destroy this fuckin' phone." Diesel hung up and called his daughter. The first time, Tori didn't answer, so he called her again. He received the same response. Defeated, he sat his phone down and fixed himself a drink. Heavy chiming from his phone made his heart rate increase.

"Tori!"

"No. It's Dazzle."

"Where's Tori?"

"She's right here."

"Let me talk to her."

"She doesn't want to talk," she stated.

"Where are you?"

"We're at North Broward Hospital."

"I'm on my way."

"I'll let her know."

Diesel grabbed the keys to his Tahoe and jogged into the living room. Byrd was sitting on the sofa, watching an episode of *First 48*. "Come drive me to the hospital."

"What happened?" Byrd jumped up with the quickness.

"Kilo was shot. I need to be up there with Tori."

Diesel sat quietly in the front seat for the twenty-minute ride. In his mind, he knew he'd fucked up. Selfish was his first name and he lived by it. Unfortunately, he often caused pain to the ones that loved him. It was in his nature, something that was embedded him since he was a young teen.

Byrd dropped him off at the entrance of the hospital. "I'm about to park. Go in there with your daughter, man."

Diesel stepped from the vehicle and slammed the door. For the second time in life, he regretted his actions because he couldn't take back his wrongdoings. Every emotion he had in his body couldn't have prepared him for the scene he was about to encounter.

The second the automatic doors opened, Diesel was greeted by loud screaming and hollering. Tori could be seen collapsing into

Eazy's arms. Rushing in their direction, he stepped between Eazy and Honcho.

"Tori, I'm here, baby." Diesel grabbed her arm.

Eazy wore the coldest, meanest mug on his face. "I don't know what for. It ain't like you give a fuck anyway," he spat.

"Out of respect for your situation, I'm going to give you a pass. I understand that you're frustrated and upset, but this is still my daughter."

"You can't give me shit. Don't be disrespectful, 'cause you know my get-down."

"You know mine too."

"So, what you wanna do?" Eazy challenged.

Honcho stepped in to diffuse the situation. "Pop! Chill out. We going through enough. Just let her go," he pulled Tori from his father's grip and hugged her tight. "Sis, whatever you need, we got you. I'll check up on you later. I love you."

Diesel took Tori into his arms and ushered her towards the exit doors. "He's gone, Daddy. He's gone," she sobbed loudly.

Guilt gripped his neck as he rubbed her shoulders. Once again, he was responsible for the death of someone his daughter loved.

Chapter 13

It had been a month since Kilo was cremated and with each passing day, Tori grew more depressed than the day he was killed. Life without him was hard and the fact that she was carrying his child made it harder. All she did was cry and drown herself in sorrow. Support was not an issue, because everyone close to her made sure she was okay. The night she left the house, Diesel took her home. One week later, she left and moved in with Eazy temporarily. In her heart, she felt like Diesel was behind the killing, but when she asked, he denied the accusations. There was no way of proving it, but that didn't mean she would let it go.

A light tap on the door interrupted her sorrow session. Before she responded, she pulled the blanket up to her neck. "Come in."

The door crept open slowly and in stepped Eazy. He was alone. In his hand, he held a bottle of orange juice. "Here."

"Sit it on the table," she whispered.

Eazy sat down on the bed and sighed heavily. Tori noticed his eyes were red, which was a clear indication he had been crying. "The detective on Kilo's case just left. They haven't made an arrest, but he dropped off some items that belonged to him. I know you want them."

Tori didn't reply. She just nodded her head. Diesel placed the plastic evidence bag on the dresser next to the orange juice.

"Tori, I know this is extremely hard for you. It's hard for me. Kilo was my firstborn. My heart. The one that made me a man. The one that taught me how to be a father. Someone took him from me and I'll never get him back."

"They took him from me too and I'll never get him back either." she sniffled. "He was my husband. We had just gotten married. We had forever to go."

"I get it. Believe me. I do."

Tori was like a daughter in his eyes. He had been in her life since she was born, so he loved her as if she was one of his children. And watching her suffer broke his heart tremendously. Gently, he rubbed her back. "Tori, I know you loved Kilo and he loved you equally. That has never been a doubt in my mind. I've watched you two develop a love so strong. Your bond was so unbreakable that no one could tear y'all apart. Not even Diesel."

"I can't live without him."

"Yes, you can. Don't say that."

"I don't want to."

"Do you think he'd be happy to see you give up on life? No. He wouldn't. Kilo would want you to move on and live your life."

"My life is incomplete without him." Tori smashed the pillow against her face and screamed as loud as her lungs allowed. "Ahh! I hate my fucking life. Why did they have to kill him?"

Eazy was a strong, violent man, but watching Tori break down made him weak. Emotions were something he tried to contain. He had to be strong for Honcho and Tori. That left little time for him to grieve.

"I can't answer that, but I wish I knew." Eazy took the pillow she was holding and pulled her into his arms. As he rocked back and forth, he tried to make it make sense.

"Moving on seems impossible right now, but trust me, you'll move on. I lost my son. My flesh and blood. He's irreplaceable. You lost the love of your life, but you'll love again. Your heart will heal, so don't give up. Your entire life is ahead of you." Eazy wiped away his tears. "I want to see you go to college. Not held up in this room like it's the end of the world."

Tori raised her head slowly and looked deep into his eyes. "You want me to leave?"

"I want you to live. Go to college, Tori. Don't throw that away. When you come back to visit, my door will be open. And once you graduate, you can move back here. I'll never push you away. You're my daughter."

Tori stopped fighting and nodded her head. "Okay."

"Just think about it, okay?"

"I will. I promise."

"Go ahead and get some rest, 'cause tomorrow I'm not letting you stay in here all day." Eazy kissed her forehead and headed for the door.

114

"Eazy?" Her new father-figure turned around and greeted her with a half-smile. "Thank you."

"You don't have to thank me. You're family."

Once Eazy was gone, Tori reached down on the side of the bed and picked up a small gift bag. Sitting it on her lap, she stuck her hand inside and pulled out a pair of gold baby booties. Engraved on the side were the words, *Baby Kingsley*. It was the Valentine's Day gift she purchased on the day he was murdered.

Seeing the booties shattered her heart all over again. Then to make matters worse, she grabbed the evidence bag and dumped the contents onto the bed. One item caught her attention. It was Kilo's diamond wedding band. Tori slipped the ring onto her necklace for safekeeping and cuddled up with Kilo's favorite pillow. For thirty minutes straight, she cried until sleep took over her body.

***

Dazzle and Fresh had been kicking it heavy since their first encounter. The two had actually become inseparable. Life at the strip club continued, being that they lost their most valuable player. Kilo's death placed a dark cloud over the city. No one was the same, including Fresh. From childhood, the two bonded tightly as friends, but over time their status eventually turned them into brothers.

"When lil man coming home?" Fresh was on the sofa playing Grand Theft Auto on the PlayStation.

"I have to pick him up from his grandma's house."

"What time you doing that?"

"Later on. Why, what's up?"

Fresh aggressively jammed his thumbs against the controller, while rocking side to side and shouting at the game. "Cheating motherfuckers!"

Dazzle was sprawled across the couch with her feet in his lap laughing at the seriousness of the video game. "Babe, what's up?"

"I'm trying to see how much nasty time we got left." His eyes never left the screen.

"As long as we want. I told her I'll pick him up on my way to work." Dazzle used her foot to rub in between his legs. "I mean, we can get started now."

"Nope! I'm playing the game right now."

"Are you serious right now?"

"Yep!"

Dazzle pouted and folded her arms. "Alright, when I fall asleep don't wake me up."

"Oh, I don't need you to be up in order for me to get some. I just need those jaw muscles relaxed and them legs open," he chuckled.

Dazzle rolled over onto her side and continued to watch him play the game. Just as she began to relax, loud banging startled the couple. "What the hell?" she uttered nervously.

"I know that ain't yo' punk ass baby daddy bangin' like that." Fresh tossed the remote on the sofa. "I hate to wet that nigga ass up."

Dazzle pulled herself from the sofa and headed towards the door in a rush. When she snatched the door open, she was surprised to see her neighbor. "What can I do for you? And why you banging on my door like I borrowed your shit and didn't return it?"

"Well, smart ass, I'm looking for Tron."

Fresh stood at his lady's side. "Aye, slow your roll. Don't come over here disrespecting my woman."

"I got this, baby." Dazzle folded her arms across her chest. "Now what the fuck do you want?"

"Is he here?" The woman peeked inside the apartment.

"No, he's not and for the last time, tell me what you want before I slam the door in your face." Dazzle's face scrunched up, displaying her irritation.

"Your baby daddy got my teenage daughter pregnant and I need to talk to him, before I send the police here to pick his ass up."

Dazzle's heart skipped a beat. "What?" Exasperation was heavy in her tone.

"Yeah. I thought that would change your tone. Now where is he?"

"I don't believe you."

"Oh, you will," she replied and looked over her shoulder. "Mya, get over here." Mya stepped into view, with her tiny frame revealing a small baby bump. It was obvious she was embarrassed by the way she avoided eye contact. "Don't be shy now. You wasn't doing all that while you was fucking in this woman's bed."

Dazzle held her hand up. "Hold the fuck up! What you mean, fucking in my bed?"

"Tell her!" Mya's mother screamed at the top of her lungs.

"I'm. I'm pregnant from Tron."

"Nah. He ain't that damn stupid." Dazzle didn't want to believe that Tron was disrespectful enough to fuck inside her house.

Mya swallowed her spit and shook her head. "It's true. We have sex when you go to work. You have dark pink Polo sheets on your bed."

"Hold on." Dazzle walked away to retrieve her phone from the table. Her fingers trembled as she pressed the send button and put it on speaker phone.

"What?" Tron picked up with an attitude.

"You that fucking nasty that you'll fuck another female in my place and in my damn bed?"

Tron huffed into the phone. "I don't know what you talking about."

"That's funny, because I have Mya and her mama here saying otherwise," Dazzle replied.

Mya's mom couldn't wait to intervene. "You about to go to jail, so I suggest you stop lying."

"Like I said, I don't know what the fuck you talking about. I haven't touched your daughter," he lied.

The fact that he wasn't owning up to his responsibility pissed her off. Without warning, she snatched the phone. Dazzle didn't react because she wanted to know the truth. "Why you on this phone lying, Tron?"

"Man, what you talking about? Why you over there starting shit?"

"I'm not starting shit. You need to quit lying and tell the truth about us and that you—" Midsentence, the screen lit up when Tron disconnected the call. When Mya handed the phone back to Dazzle, she snatched it from her.

"Y'all can leave now. Oh, and if you decide to call the police, don't send them to my place. You better go and find Tron." Dazzle slammed the door in both of their faces.

Fresh sat up and folded his hands. "You good, baby?"

"No."

"What you need me to do?"

Dazzle stood in front of him and grabbed both of his hands. "I need some dick."

Fresh bit his bottom lip and grinned. "I think I can help you with that."

"Good. Come on." Fresh rose to his feet and the two of them made their way to the bedroom.

Chapter 14
Georgia State University
Atlanta, GA

Tori was knocked out when she felt someone shake her. The bright light from the room damn near blinded her. Laced with confusion, she blinked repeatedly as she looked around the room. In front of her stood Professor Gordon.

"Class is over."

"Thanks." Tori grabbed her book and shoved it inside her JanSport backpack.

"Is everything okay with you Tori? You've been sleeping a lot in class lately."

"Yes. I'm just tired."

"You sure about that?" Professor Gordon was a tall, brown-skinned woman with short, curly hair.

Tori nodded her head. "I'm sure."

Professor Gordon sat down at the empty desk beside her. "Can I ask you a question?"

"Sure."

"Are you pregnant?" Tori hesitated. That was one question she wasn't prepared to answer. "You don't have to be afraid to answer that. I want to help you. There is so much potential inside of you and I don't want to see you lose it."

"Yes," she whispered.

Every emotion she held inside was strangling her. The thought of being a single mother was something she never thought she would have to face. Kilo wanted to be a father, but someone robbed him of that far too early. A stream of tears flooded her brown cheeks. "I don't know what do."

"Is it because the father wants nothing to do with the baby?"

Tori used the sleeve of her sweater to wipe the tears from her face. "He was murdered."

Professor Gordon's mouth hung open. The news saddened her instantly. She placed her hand on Tori's shoulder. "I'm so sorry Tori. Is there anything that you need me to help you with?"

"No. I just need some advice. I'm so lost right now."

"Are you ready to take on the responsibility of being a mother? That's a hard task, especially while you're in school." Tori shrugged her shoulders. "If you're not ready, you have other options, such as giving the child up for adoption."

"I've thought about that or having an abortion, but I'm just not sure on which is the best option."

Professor Gordon stared at the white board in deep thought with glassy eyes. "A few years ago, someone close to me had been trying to have a baby for the longest time. She tried everything under the sun. Nothing seemed to work for her. Then one day, she finally got that positive test result she was waiting on." The professor paused and wiped her face.

"What happened?" Tori was anxious.

"By the time she was four months, the doctor told her she had to make a decision. She had to choose her life or her baby's life." She sniffled and looked over at Tori. "She chose the baby. But sadly, she went into labor early and died during childbirth."

"I'm so sorry to hear that."

"Thank you."

"What happened to the baby?"

"The baby died also."

Tori was completely saddened by her story, but she needed more. "Why are you telling me this?"

"Because there are people in the world that desire nothing more than to become a mother. I don't believe in abortions. However, it's your decision and you're the only person that knows your situation. All I'm saying is to weigh your options before you make your final decision. Confide in your family about your decision, since they're the ones who will have your back in this."

"I will." Tori looked down at her watch. "I'm sorry, but I have to go to my next class. Thank you for the advice. I really appreciate it."

"You're welcome."

Tori grabbed her things and left the classroom in a hurry. It was three o'clock in the afternoon, so she didn't have any classes left. On her way through the glass doors, she scurried through the parking lot to find her car.

Downtown was always crowded. Tori pushed through the busy traffic until she reached her destination fifteen minutes later. Pulling up in the parking lot, she put the car in park and took off her seatbelt. The pressure she felt was too much for her young heart. Tori looked down at the diamond ring on her finger.

"Kilo, baby, why did you have to leave me so soon? I'm so lost without you and I don't know what to do. A part of me wants to keep our baby, but I know I can't do this alone. Tell me what to do, please."

Tori leaned back against the headrest and closed her eyes. "God, please help me. Show me a sign. I'm so lost. There's no way I could be a good mother under these type of conditions. I still have four years left of school. That's going to be difficult for me."

After sitting in the parking lot for thirty minutes just staring at the abortion clinic, Tori made a decision to get out the car. As much as she wanted to keep his legacy alive, it just wasn't possible. Tori stepped out the car and looked up into the sky.

"Kilo, I'm sorry, baby. Please don't be upset with me, but I'm doing what's best for me." Tori closed the door and casually walked towards the entrance. The decision she made was going to haunt her for the rest of her life, but her reasoning was logical. There was no way she could raise their child. She just hoped that God forgave her in the end.

***

Dazzle packed a bag for Jamir. "Come on, baby. Let's go."

Jamir sat down on the bed with a cute little frown and arms folded. "I don't want to go over there."

"Why not, baby? I thought you liked being at your grandmother's house, so you can play with your cousins."

"We don't be over there."

"Oh." Dazzle was a little unsettled, so she sat down beside her son. "Well, where does your dad take you when I drop you off?"

"We stay at Auntie Tweety house."

Dazzle's heartrate increased by the millisecond. "What? What do you mean you be at Auntie Tweety's house?"

Jamir looked up with his big, brown eyes beaming. "Dad lives with Auntie Tweety."

It took everything in her to keep calm in front of her son. "I'll be right back, okay? Just watch the Disney channel."

"Okay." Dazzle left his room and closed the door. Rushing into the living room, she picked up her phone and called Lala.

"What's up, girl?"

Dazzle cut straight to the chase. "You won't believe the shit I just heard."

"What?"

"Please tell me why Jamir just told me that Tron is living with Tweety."

Lala had a puzzled look on her face. "I know you lying."

"I'm about to find out, but I know my baby telling the truth." Unable to sit down, she paced the floor. "I told him I was about to drop him off to his grandma house and he told me he didn't want to go to Auntie Tweety's house."

"Damn! That's fucked up if he is. Let Tweety tell it, she can't stand his ass."

"Oh, I know. She was the same one telling me that I should leave him because he ain't shit."

"Yeah, so her ass can be with his ain't shit ass."

"I' m about to go over there and find out on my own." Dazzle checked her purse for the can of mace she carried. "If he over there, I'm beating Tweety's ass."

"Not by yourself, you ain't. I'll meet you over there." Lala got up from the sofa and put on her shoes.

"I'm about to leave my house now." Dazzle walked back to Jamir's room. "Come on, baby. Let's go." That time, he got up without a fight.

It only took fifteen minutes for Dazzle to arrive at Tweety's apartment in the shallow side neighborhood. Just as she parked the car, she spotted Lala pulling into the complex as well. The way the building was set up, no one could spot the cars from the window.

Lala got out the car and approached Dazzle, swinging a bat in her hand. Peeking inside the window, she scratched her scalp. "You brought the baby with you."

"Yep! I didn't have time to drop him off."

"Well, let's go. I wanna see what she have to say about this." Lala stood back on her legs with her hands on her hips. Dazzle opened up the back door and took Jamir out of his car seat. Then she reached inside her purse and grabbed the mace.

Normally, the complex had activity going on. But that particular day, it was quiet. They all rode the elevator to the third floor and got off. As they approached Tweety's door, they were greeted by slimy ass Tron. He froze like a deer in headlights.

"What? What—" That was all he could get out his mouth.

"Don't stutter now, bitch! You fucking Tweety?" Dazzle spat.

"I don't know what you talking about," Tron lied.

"Stop lying. I know you live here, dummy." Dazzle had her hand clutched tightly around the mace.

"Bae, who you—" Tweety stopped midsentence the second she saw Dazzle and Lala standing at her front door.

"Bae! Oh, y'all together." Dazzle was furious and there was no more controlling her actions. She whipped out the mace and sprayed Tron in the face with it.

"Aaargghh! You bitch." Tron stumbled backwards with his hands covering his face.

Tweety tried to close the door, but Dazzle kicked it and it hit her in the face. "You dirty ass hoe."

Tweety was dazed and her head was pounding, but that didn't stop Dazzle from getting on her ass. Dazzle swung on her twice, striking her in the face. It was a flat-out brawl after that. Lala grabbed Jamir and took him inside the bedroom. "Stay in here until I come back."

Lala went back into the living room where the fight was taking place. Behind her, she could hear water running. When she walked towards the kitchen, Lala saw Tron washing his face. Dazzle was on top of Tweety, banging her head against the floor. "You stupid ass bitch."

Lala felt someone behind her, so she turned around. Tron brushed past her and tried to break up the fight. He snatched Dazzle by her weave and Lala went crazy on his ass with the bat. Wildly, she swung at his legs and arms, cracking bones in the process.

"Call the police!" Lala heard someone scream.

Immediately, she grabbed Dazzle by the arm. "We gotta go. Get Jamir from out the room." Dazzle rushed into the room and snatched up her son. The three of them were able to flee without being seen by the police, who flew into the complex with the sirens blaring.

***

Inside the apartment, Tweety was trying to help Tron flush the toxic chemical from his eyes, when there was loud banging on the door. "Police! Open up!"

Tweety panicked instantly. "Shit, Tron! What the fuck we supposed to do?"

"Just open the door. You already know one of these nosy ass neighbors called them folks." Tron leaned against the sink, dabbing his eyes with the milk-soaked rag.

Tweety dragged slowly to the door and opened it. "Yes, Officer? How can I help you?"

"We received a call about a fight that took place in this apartment." The officer peeked inside the apartment.

"No. There was no disturbance."

"Care to explain the bruises on your face?" Crossing the threshold, he signaled for his partners to follow. "Step aside, ma'am. We need to see who else is in here."

The officers bombarded her space and began to question Tron. "What's your name, sir?"

"Antron Davis." There was no hesitation in his response, since he didn't have any warrants in his name.

"And yours, ma'am?"

"Davina Ingram."

The officer extended his arm towards the sofa. "Come over here and have a seat while we run your names." Tweety and Tron sat down across from each other. Instantly, Tron began to sweat from nervousness. On the television stand, he spotted the handgun that he was supposed to put away, but it'd slipped his mind.

Officer Douchebag was scoping out the area when his eyes landed on the weapon. He reached into his back pocket and pulled out a handkerchief. "Who does this belong to?"

Fear pumped through Tweety's heart as she looked at Tron. He dropped his head because he knew what time it was. "Mine," he mumbled.

"You're a convicted felon, sir. So, you know what that means." The officer removed his cuffs. "Antron Davis, I need you to stand up and put your hands behind your back."

The officer read Tron his rights before he hauled him off to be detained. Tweety sat on the sofa, crying her eyes out.

Chapter 15
Four years later

The sound of the alarm going off pulled Tori from a sound, peaceful sleep. Happily, she sprung from the bed with a huge smile on her face and rushed into the bathroom. Turning on the shower, she stripped out the t-shirt she wore and stepped into the hot shower. Water trickled over her body, as she lathered up her washcloth. Thoroughly, she bathed twice before stepping back out.

Tori stood in the full body mirror while applying her lotion. When she reached the side of her arm, a lump formed in her throat. Embedded on her right arm was a portrait of Kilo's face. "I did it, baby. I graduated with my bachelor's degree in accounting."

Moving to her left arm, she smiled at the tattooed baby blocks that read, *Capone.* "Mommy did it, baby boy. I'll never forget about you. I love you so much."

A teary eyed Tori left the bathroom and got dressed quickly, while giving herself a pep talk. "No tears today. You've reached a milestone and you should be happy."

Just then, her phone vibrated against the wooden nightstand. Already aware of who was calling, she rushed to pick it up. "Hello."

"Hey, girl. Where you at?" Marcy asked.

"Home, but I'm about to leave out now. Where are you?"

"I'm leaving out too."

"Okay. Well, I'll see you shortly."

Tori hung up the phone, then she grabbed her cap and gown before rushing out the door. It was early in the morning, so the Atlanta traffic was a breeze. Upon her arrival, the parking lot was quite empty.

Inside the building, the graduating class stood around the auditorium, preparing to walk the stage. Tori walked around until she met up with her classmates. Marcy greeted her with a big hug. "We did it. Are you excited?"

"Hell, yeah. I never thought I would see this day."

"Me either. We have been through hell and high water together. I'm just happy that it's over. So, we hanging out after this?"

"Actually, I have a flight to catch when it's over. I'm going back to Florida tonight."

Marcy frowned with disappointment. "You're leaving? As in not coming back?"

"No, I'll be back. You know I can't leave until my lease is up."

"Yeah. That's true."

Professor Gordon could be heard over the microphone, clearing her throat. "Attention! Graduates, we're about to open the doors. So, please find your seats. The students that are giving speeches please report to the stage. Thank you."

Marcy smiled and grabbed Tori's arm. "That would be us."

"I guess it is."

Tori took a seat and prepared herself for the long, boring ceremony. Hopefully, the time would fly by and it would be over quicker than she anticipated.

Two and a half hours later

"At this time, I would like to introduce the Valedictorian for the class of 2015. This student has overcome many obstacles over the years and I would like to commend her for a job well done. No matter what she went through, she managed to maintain an 'A' average. Today, she will walk the stage with a 5.0 GPA. Without further ado, put your hands together for Tori Price."

The auditorium was filled with thunderous claps. Filled with nothing but joy, Tori stood up and took her place at the podium. As she looked out into the crowd, she teared up instantly. There was one person she wished could be in attendance, and in physical form at that. Taking a deep breath, she exhaled and began her speech.

"Thank you, everybody. This is the most exciting day of my life. It symbolizes my growth, success and a new beginning.

During my first semester, I didn't think that I would make it because I was grieving." Tori paused and wiped away the single tear streaming down her cheek. "Four years ago, I lost someone that meant the world to me and my life hasn't been the same. Each day it gets harder, but I can honestly stand here and say this is the happiest day of my life. I know he's shining down on me." Tori looked up at the ceiling. "I know you're looking down on me. In fact, I know you're in this building, along with my mommy."

Tori then looked out into the crowd. "I did it and I excelled. It wasn't easy, but it was worth it. It's an honor to announce that I'm a part of the 2015 graduating class. Congratulations to us, as we start our new journey. Thank you."

Once the commencement ceremony was over, Tori mingled with her friends for a little bit, then headed out the door. As she walked out the glass door, she stopped in her tracks. Standing in her presence was an unexpected visitor.

"Congratulations, baby. I'm so proud of you." Diesel stood there with some beautiful, red roses.

"You came."

"I wouldn't have missed this for the world," he expressed while passing her the flowers. "I heard your speech. You did an awesome job. I'm so proud of you, Tori."

"Thank you." Diesel noticed the glassiness in her eyes. So, he pulled her close and embraced his baby girl. "It's okay. Everything is going to be okay. We're about to celebrate. I'm taking you to dinner. We can go wherever you want to go."

"Well, let's go. I'm hungry." It was such a joy to have her father's support on her big day. Over the last few years, their relationship had improved. No doubt, it wasn't perfect, but they were taking steps in the right direction.

Tori decided on Mary Mac's Tea Room, so that's where they ended up. The establishment wasn't crowded as yet, but it was filling up nicely as the other graduates popped up.

"Good afternoon, sir. How many?"

"Umm. A table for four. I would like a booth seat."

"Okay. Give me one moment. I'll be right back," she replied.

Tori cut her eyes in Diesel's direction with a bit of confusion on her face. "Why do we need a table for four? Who did you bring with you?"

Diesel hesitated at first. You'll see in a few minutes."

Just then the waitress reappeared. "Right this way please."

They were seated in a corner booth on the far end of the restaurant. Tori sat there, anxiously waiting to see who was about to join them. While they waited, the two engaged in small talk.

"So, what are your plans, now that you've graduated?" Diesel asked, while sipping on his sweet tea.

Tori twirled her silverware in a glass of hot water. "Honestly, I don't know what I want to do. The accounting firm I did my externship with offered me a job here in the city."

"That means you haven't accepted it yet."

"No."

"You don't want to live here?"

Tori sighed. "Not exactly. I want to come back home, but what am I coming back to?"

Diesel's face balled up instantly. "Me. What do you mean?"

"Nothing," she shook her head. "It's just a lot to think about. The thought of coming back to face my reality is hard. It makes my chest tight when I think about it."

"In life we have to accept the fact that we will reach our demise. We just don't know the day or hour. You have to come to terms that no matter what, you have to move on. Do you think he would want you moping around and giving up on life? No. Life is too short to be depressed and living in the past. You have to find your happiness."

From Tori's peripheral view, she could see a human figure walk up to their table. Diesel looked nervous, so she turned to see who was standing beside her. The woman at her side was someone she had never seen a day in her life. Nor was the little boy. However, Diesel knew exactly who they were. Standing up from his seat, he allowed the woman and child to climb inside.

Tori began to fume and it was evident by the way she rocked in her seat with a mean mug on her face. Diesel knew he needed to start talking. "I know this is awkward, but I thought this was a good time to introduce them to you. This is Jenna and we've been dating for a while now. And this is—"

Tori cut him off with the quickness. "Let me take a wild guess. He's your son?" Her eyes never left the little boy who was a spitting image of her father.

Diesel lowered his gaze. "Yes. This is Torin Jr., your little brother."

"How old is he?"

"I'm eight," Torin spoke up quickly. "I always wanted a big sister."

Ignoring his comment, she shifted her focus back to her deceitful father. "So, let me get this straight. He's eight. My mom has been dead for seven years, which means you were cheating on her while the two of you were married." Tori's eyes instantly watered. "And to make matters worse, you allowed her to make him a junior, when my little brother was killed because of you. He was your fuckin' junior," she screamed. "I know Mommy is flipping in her grave off this shit."

Those words crushed his heart. "Tori, I can explain. Please, don't do this. I've wanted to tell you for the longest time, but the timing was always wrong," he pleaded.

"You know what, Diesel, don't bother." Tori grabbed her purse from the seat.

"Don't leave. Let's talk as a family."

"No thank you. Enjoy your family in peace. My family is already dead and gone." Tori's eyes had turned into venomous slits. "Enjoy *your* family. I have a flight to catch."

Tori left the restaurant angry and with a broken heart. For years, she had questioned Diesel's feelings towards her mother. The impromptu meeting was confirmation he didn't love her mother the way he claimed he did. On her way back to her apartment, she contemplated on her next move. There was no way she was going back to live with Diesel. That was a well-known fact. Regardless of where she chose to reside, her mind was made up and to become the Queen of the Trap, wherever that was.

Chapter 16

Later on that night, Tori exited the sliding glass doors at the Ft. Lauderdale-Hollywood International Airport. Freshness was in the air, as she inhaled the sweet swell of South Florida. "Home sweet home. Damn, it feels good to be here."

The night air caused her hair to flow in the gentle breeze. Everyone walked at a fast pace, while she stood in place taking it all in. Just then the sound of a horn interrupted her thoughts. Loud screaming and shouting could be heard right after. Lala and Dazzle were running directly towards her.

"Tori! Tori!" they shouted, while giving her a tight hug.

"Hey!" She smiled. "I missed y'all so much."

"We missed you too."

Dazzle backed up and looked her up and down. "You look good sis."

"Thanks, girl. Y'all do too."

"Well, let's go. We have so much catching up to do." Dazzle grabbed one of Tori's bags and went to the car. Once the trunk was loaded, they pulled off.

"So, what's going on with y'all?" Tori asked from the passenger seat.

Dazzle shrugged her shoulders. "Shit. Just waiting to get off damn probation."

"Damn, how much longer do you have?" Tori quizzed.

"One year and it's over."

"I thought you was off of that by now."

"I wish, but at least my P.O. cool as fuck. He don't harass me or nothing like that. I pay my restitution and keep it pushing."

"Tron still locked up?"

"Yep." She exhaled. "Please don't talk that fuck nigga up," she laughed. Dazzle eased the car onto I-595 and slid soft.

***

"So, are you in the mood to go out tonight?" Lala was on the floor doing a split.

"From the look of things, it seems as if you've taken Dazzle's place on the stripper pole." Tori joked.

"No! I just need something hard and stiff right now." With her legs extending east and west, she stretched her arms out in front of her, lowering her chest to the tile. "And since Honcho won't be back in town for a few weeks, I have to find someone else to do."

"Really, hoe!" Tori giggled. "You cheating on Honcho?"

"Technically, no! We're not a couple. The man lives in Atlanta and I have no idea who's fucking and sucking on him while he's home. Therefore, I will continue to do me until our circumstances change."

"I guess I should mind my own business then." Tori covered her mouth as she yawned. In reality she was tired, but there was no way she was declining an opportunity to go out and have some fun.

"I think you should wake up and get ready for a night of fun." Lala closed her legs and stood to her feet.

"I'm ready. We just waiting on slow ass Dazzle to come out. She in there trying to get her back blew out before we leave." Tori and Lala laughed hysterically.

"You a lie. I was slobbing on that knob." Dazzle hit the corner with her tongue out, twerking to no music.

"Remind me to not drink or smoke behind you." Lala grabbed her purse off the couch.

"My nigga!" Fresh walked out with a huge grin on his face. "Damn, it's been a long ass time."

Tori stood up and gave Fresh a hug. "What's up? I heard you been treating my girl good."

"You know I wanted her for a long time. So, I had to make it worth her wild." Fresh took a step back and smiled. "Damn, sis, you cut the fuck up on that tattoo of my brother. That bitch hard as fuck." He grabbed her arm to get a better look at the other tattoo. "Capone?" His brow furrowed in confusion. "Who is that?"

Tori looked away and closed her eyes to suppress the tears that wanted to fall so bad. A deep breath escaped her lips. When she opened her eyes Fresh, Dazzle and Lala were staring at her. In slow motion she opened her mouth and let the words fall painfully. "Right before Kilo was killed, I found out I was pregnant. I planned on telling him, but I didn't get the chance to. While I held him in my arms, he told me to name our son Capone." A few tears started to fall, but she quickly wiped her face. "He knew. He found my pregnancy test underneath the cabinet."

"Damn, sis!" Fresh held her in his arms tightly and rubbed her back. "I'm sorry. I know this is hard for you. The love y'all shared was real. I know you loved bro to death and he loved you the same way. That nigga was so ready to marry you, we couldn't even come to the courthouse with y'all. Shit, I was waiting for a wedding, not a funeral."

"Me too," she sniffled. "Life is so unfair. I'll never find anyone else like him. That was my only shot at happiness."

"It feels like that right now, but you'll find someone else to make you happy. Not like Kilo, but don't give up just yet."

Lala stepped in closer with her eyes on Tori. The glassiness that covered her pupils, displayed the hurt. "What happened to the baby?"

"I had to get rid of it. There was no way I could take care of a child in my predicament. It was a hard decision, but I didn't have any other choices," she pleaded.

"It's okay. No judgment here." Lala used her thumbs to wipe away Tori's tears. "No more crying. For the night any way," she laughed. "Today was your big day, so it's time for us to go and celebrate."

"Yes, please, let's do that." Dazzle turned and placed a kiss on Fresh's cheek. "I'll see you when I get back."

"Be safe."

"We will." Fresh walked the girls outside and stood there until they pulled out the driveway. When he turned around, Jamir was standing in the doorway. "It's just me and you, man." Fresh went inside and closed the door behind them.

***

The club was packed when they arrived. Every dope boy and check boy was in the building representing their hoods. Of course, they were easy to spot, rocking their expensive clothing and jewelry.

"Go to the bar," Dazzle shouted over the music.

The girls bumped their way through the crowd. Some moved easily and the drunk dudes were grabbing their arms a little too aggressively. Tori tried to keep her cool, as she slapped away someone's hand. "Don't touch me," she snapped.

Tori spotted a familiar face, but she looked away. Jarvis was the last one she wanted to see. If it wasn't for him running his mouth, Diesel would've never known about her business in the first place. A group of girls turned to face them as they waited to take their spot. One looked at Tori and smiled. "Hey, Tori. When did you get back?"

"A few hours ago."

"It's good to see you. We should catch up one day," Whitney suggested, while giving her a hug.

"Yeah. We can do that."

"Is your number still the same?"

"Yeah."

"Okay. I'll hit you up."

"Cool."

Lala couldn't wait for them to walk away. "Uhh, who is that?"

"Why? Are you jealous?" Tori laughed.

"Hell no. But we don't need no damn replacement and we ain't accepting applications either." Lala rolled her eyes.

"That's Whitney. She lives next door to Kilo's dad." Tori waved the bartender in their direction.

"Tuh!" Lala huffed. "I know you better not be talking to nobody that had any dealings with Honcho."

"Why you so stupid?" Dazzle laughed. "I swear, you are childish as fuck. Where did all of that come from?"

"Let me be childish, but I mean that shit."

Before Tori could respond, the bartender was standing in front of her. "What can I get for you?"

"Let me get an Amaretto Sour and two Long Island Iced Teas." Tori then turned to look at a frowning Lala. "To ease your curiosity, Whitney likes white boys. She doesn't do hood niggas. Now you can relax."

"Good." The bartender sat their drinks down and collected her money before she moved on to help the next patron.

One hour later, the girls hit the dance floor. The alcohol in their system had them loose and ready to party. Tori found herself dancing with a dude she'd recognized in passing around the hood. For the first time, she was able to enjoy herself without feeling guilty. It always felt like Kilo was frowning when she attempted to enjoy herself. Not tonight though.

All of a sudden, the DJ switched up the music and played "Spend The Night" by Plies. "I think I'm making some love connections tonight," the DJ shouted over the microphone.

Handsome whispered in Tori's ear. "You hear that?"

"Hear what?" she slurred while continuing to grind against his crotch, as his hands rested on her hips.

"Baby wanna spend the night." He kissed her neck.

Tori was lit and the warmth of his lips on her flesh turned her on. It had been four years since she slept with anyone, so she was vulnerable. However, she had to stay strong. "I don't even know you like that to be going home with you."

"We can get to know each other. What you wanna know?" he whispered.

"First off, we can start with your name."

"Jude."

Tori nodded her head. That name definitely rang a bell in her head. "Jude. I've heard about you in the streets."

"Hopefully, it was all good."

"I guess so."

Truth be told, she'd heard he sold dope. Jude wasn't a kingpin, but he was feared in the streets. His bad boy demeanor wasn't new to her. Kilo was definitely on a higher pedestal than Jude. With plans to step back into the dope game she needed protection.

Last call for alcohol was announced, so Tori stopped dancing and looked around for Dazzle and Lala. When she saw them, they were leaning against the wall. Tori turned to face Jude. "I'm about to go over here and talk to my girls."

"What you about to tell them, you sliding with me?"

Tori placed her hand on his firm chest. *Damn*, she thought to herself. "Only if you promise not to do anything to me."

"I won't do nothing you don't want me to do." Jude took another look at Tori and licked his lips. "Tell them we leaving."

"Okay."

Lala and Dazzle looked hot and irritated. "Y'all good?" Tori asked.

"Shit, we ready to go." Dazzle wiped her face.

"Me too," Tori added.

"Well, let's go." Lala stood straight up.

"I'm going with Jude," Tori blurted out.

"Jude?" Dazzle cut her eyes. "The nigga you been dancing with?"

"Yeah. Why you say it like that?"

"Uhh, because I don't know him." Dazzle wanted her girl to have fun, but she didn't feel comfortable letting her leave with the nigga. True enough, she knew of him, but she didn't know Jude and he damn sure didn't know crazy ass Diesel.

On the other hand, Lala was cool with it. "Girl, do you. He is fine. Just be safe, shit."

"I will. I'll text y'all. Bye."

"We leaving too." Lala and Dazzle followed Tori back over to where Jude was standing.

"I'm ready." They all headed towards the exit.

Dazzle couldn't wait until they got out into the parking lot. She stepped in front of Jude. "Umm. I don't really feel comfortable with my sister leaving with you, but she's grown."

Jude cut her off. "Don't worry. I'm not going to bring any harm her way. She in good hands," he promised.

"Good, because we," she waved her finger between her and Lala, "crazy and so is her daddy, Diesel. He'll kill you if you do anything to his daughter."

Jude thought it was cute how Dazzle was so overprotective of her sister. "Trust me, I know all about her daddy." He held his hands up in defense. "And I don't need those type of problems. I'm just trying to get to know her a little more, that's all."

Dazzle decided to not take it any further. She hugged Tori. "Text me later."

"I will."

"Me too." Lala hugged her favorite girl. "I love you, sis."

"I love you too."

After parting ways, Tori followed Jude to a black, two-door Cadillac CTS. Posing as the perfect gentleman, he opened the door so she could get inside. Jude then went to the driver's side and climbed in. When he fired up the engine, the sound of "Everythang" by Young Jeezy blared through the speakers.

Jude rapped to the beat, as he peeled out the parking lot like he was on runway. Intoxicated or not, Tori slid on her seat belt. The sudden movement made Jude look over into the passenger seat. It was obvious to him that she was concerned about her safety. Using his right hand, he turned down the volume, then placed it on her knee. "My bad, baby. I'll slow down."

Tori nodded her head up and down. "I would appreciate that."

"You hungry? You wanna go to Waffle House?" His speech was a little slurred.

"No. I'm not hungry. I wanna lay down."

"Cool."

Jude slid onto I-95 south, leaving left Boca Raton. Tori looked out the window in silence during the entire ride. Fifteen minutes later, he got off on Commercial Boulevard. Eventually, the two ended up at the apartment complex on 44th Street. He used his gate card to gain access.

Inside the apartment, Tori was impressed with his cleanliness. It was definitely a bachelor pad. "Your place looks nice."

Jude's eyes wouldn't leave her breasts. He was so intoxicated by her sex appeal and she wasn't even trying. "You should see my bedroom."

Tori laughed it off. "Slow down, tiger. Where's the bathroom?"

"Straight down the hallway."

Tori went inside the bathroom and locked the door. Quickly, she shot a text message to Dazzle and Lala just in case she needed back-up. The mace she carried inside her purse would only go so far.

Upon re-entering the living room, she saw Jude sitting on the sofa rolling up a blunt. Tori sat down beside him. "So, what's your game plan, Jude? Why did you want to bring me home with you?"

"Shit, I'm just trying to get to know you."

Tori crossed her legs and looked deeply into his low, brown eyes. "Be honest. You want to fuck me, don't you?"

Immediately, Jude started laughing. Then he placed the blunt between his lips and lit it. Taking a long pull, he allowed the smoke to fill his lungs. Jude released the smoke that didn't go up his nose into the air. "Damn, you cut straight to the chase, huh?"

Tori leaned back against the sofa. "I mean, we are adults and I just want to know what's your intentions with me tonight?"

Jude wasn't sure if that was a trick question or what, but in his eyes, there was no point in lying. "I mean, why wouldn't I want to? But I don't want you to think that's the only reason I wanted you here. It's more to it to that."

"Yeah, yeah. You want to get to know me. I get it." Tori rolled her eyes and sucked her teeth.

"You wanna know the truth?"

"Of course."

Jude sat his blunt down on the smoke tray. "A few years back, I had the biggest crush on you."

Tori was shocked to say the least. "Oh really?"

"Most definitely."

"Gotcha!" The sarcasm was heavy.

"Dead ass. I used to see you running the streets with Kilo." The sound of his name increased the beating of her heart. "When he got locked up, I wanted to get at you so bad. But one of your workers told me you wasn't having it."

"And who would that be?"

"Jarvis," he replied.

The sound of his name disgusted her. "I should've known. What, you cool with him or something?"

"Nah. I don't know that lil' hotheaded nigga. You used to pull up on him at the store, that's what made me approach him."

"Oh, okay."

"You wanna hit this?"

"Yeah." Tori took the blunt from Jude and took a pull. The smoke made her cough the first time around, but the more she hit it, the easier it became. Before she knew it, the room started to spin.

Chapter 17

Lala was buzzing heavy and feeling a little frisky. "I want you to come with me to this nigga house. He always bragging about how much money he got and how many inches he packing."

Dazzle was in her zone as well. "Shit, let's go…shit. I feel like getting in a little trouble tonight anyway."

Lala's eyes widened in excitement. "For real? You gone go with me?"

"Hell yeah. I'm not stripping anymore and I could use the extra money. Fresh been hustling, but shit has gotten tight since he bought this house."

Lala reached down and grabbed her phone from the middle console. "If I didn't know any better, I would think that you were mad that he bought it."

"No, I'm happy he bought the house. All I ever wanted was for my baby to have his own backyard."

"Just checking." Lala scrolled through her phone and pressed send.

"I know it's a God, if you calling my phone this time of time of night." Terry laughed into the phone.

"Must be. Where you at?"

"Home. Why, you trying to come over?" Terry was on the opposite end of the phone stroking his piece to the sound of her voice.

"Duhhh! That's why I'm calling."

"You always got some slick coming out that mouth." Terry licked his lips. "I have something to put in it though."

"We'll see about that. I'm on my way."

"Hurry up and bring your pretty ass over here," Terry replied.

"I will. Get your hand out your boxers and don't start without me." Lala smirked. She already knew what time it was with him. Whenever he masturbated with her on the phone, his voice deepened.

"You think you know me."

"I do. You're so predictable. Bye."

Twenty-five minutes later, Lala pulled up to a house parked in a dead end. The street lights were barely lit, but Terry's porch light was on. Lala parked the car and removed the keys from the ignition.

"We're here. Let's get this nigga money."

"Let's do it."

Dazzle walked behind Lala and stood on the front porch, while she knocked. Not even a minute later, the door opened and Terry stood there in a silk robe and a pair of boxers. The sight of both women made him rock up instantly.

"Damn, this gotta be a nigga lucky night." He stroked his goatee.

"You gone stand there and slob, or you gone let us in?" Lala pushed past him and stepped inside.

Terry closed the door and locked it. "So, who is this?" He was staring at Dazzle's ass poking through her skirt.

"This is my friend, Dee."

Terry grabbed her hand and kissed it. "Nice to meet you, new friend. You are a beautiful sight for sore eyes."

"Thank you."

"Can I get you ladies something to drink?" Terry asked.

"Yeah. What you got?"

"Grey Goose."

"I hope you have some chaser for that," Lala said, following him into the kitchen. "Come on, Dee."

"As a matter of fact, I do."

Dazzle and Lala sat on the stools while he fixed them a drink. "We want pineapple juice," Lala spoke up.

Terry poured up the drinks and slid each girl her glass. Then he fixed himself one. Holding it up in the air, he smiled. "Here's a toast for a good night." Their glasses clinked.

After spending some time in the kitchen, they took the party into the bedroom. Lala stood at the foot of the bed and removed her fitted jeans, along with her half-shirt. Her C-cup breasts sat up nicely in her black satin bra.

"Damn, girl. You been keeping all that good shit from me, huh?" Terry walked over to his nightstand and pulled out a plate of coke. "Do y'all girls party?"

Dazzle shot Lala a puzzling look. In her mind she was thinking, *bitch are you crazy?* Instead of replying, she remained silent to see what Lala was going to say.

"Nope. We don't mess with that white girl but do your thang, boo. We gone smoke this weed." Lala nodded in Dazzle's direction. "Girl, get comfortable."

Dazzle slowly, yet seductively removed her top and skirt. Terry's eyes almost burst from the sockets when he saw her standing there in a thong and bra. "Damn, that's a stallion right there." Dazzle was thick in all the right places.

"Sounds like you want some of this?" Dazzle flirted. It had been a while since she worked at the strip club, but she still had it in her.

"So, again, I get to have both of y'all?" Terry prayed silently in his head he'd get to fuck two beauties in one night.

Terry had been begging Lala for some pussy since he met her eighth months ago. Under any other circumstances, had it been another chick, he would've taken the pussy like he'd done on multiple occasions. But he was never arrested for it. His victims never said a word when he shoved money in their faces and threw them outside like yesterday's trash. However, there was something about Lala that kept him intrigued and patient.

"Of course you do. That's why we're here." Lala pushed him onto the bed. "Let me see you snort that." She handed him the powder sack on the nightstand.

Terry was excited. He dumped the powder onto the mirror that sat beside him and sucked up the white substance like a vacuum. "Whoo! Shit!" Pinching the bridge of his nose, Terry coughed violently. "This some good shit." his red, watery eyes landed on Lala. "You sure you don't want to hit this?"

Quickly irritated, she moved the blunt from her lips. "For the last time, we don't do no damn coke. Knock yourself out."

Dazzle snatched the weed from Lala's fingertips. "It's time to get busy," she stated softly.

Meanwhile, Terry was having a solo snort party. After each line, he took a shot of whiskey. He was so zoned out that he didn't realize Lala was standing in front of him wearing her birthday suit. She needed him to focus, so she looked around the room. In the corner, a wooden paddle caught her eye. Lala grabbed the paddle and turned around. Terry was now standing on his feet, leaned forward with his head back on the glass. Using the paddle, she whacked him across his ass. *Whap!*

Terry stood straight up and shouted. "What the hell?"

"Climb up on that bed. You said you was a freak. Now show me. Get ya ass on that bed."

Whap! Lala struck him again.

"Yo' ass tripping, girl. I'm the one that does the paddling."

"It's my way or no way." Terry did as he was told and leaned forward against the bed. Lala paddled him until his cheeks were red. Afterwards, she pushed him out the way and laid down on the bed. "Are you hungry, Terry?"

"Hell yeah," he grinned, while rubbing his hands together.

"Well, eat. Come on, Dee."

Dazzle laid beside Lala on the bed and opened her legs. Terry moved back and forth, feasting on two sets of goodies. He even dumped a little powder on them to make things a little more interesting. Ultimately, he ended up with one straddling his face, while the other one rode him until he reached his peak.

Terry was knocked the fuck out when it was all over. Lala and Dazzle got up to take a shower and get dressed. "He keeps his money and drugs in a bag in his closet. I'm about to grab that and then we can leave."

"Good. Fresh done called me twice and I need to get home." Dazzle's tone was soft. "I'm about to go out in the living room and call him back."

Lala went inside the closet and grabbed the bag. Tossing it over her shoulder, she backed up and bumped into the rack. Suddenly, the top shelf fell and crashed against the floor. She tried her best to remain quiet. As she walked out the closet, Terry was standing at the door in a pair of boxers. His eyes turned into demonic slits.

"What the fuck you doing in my shit?"

"I. Um. Um…" She was busted and didn't know how to lie her way out of it.

"You stealing from me?"

"No. We just wanted some weed."

"Weed, huh?" He laughed, but it was evil and it sent chills down her spine. "Okay." Terry grabbed Lala by the shoulders and slung her onto the floor. "Bitch, you must be out your rabbit ass mind if you think I believe that shit."

Terry slapped Lala across the face. She let out a loud scream, as he began to choke her. The weight of his body on top of her made it hard to throw him off. From the corner of her eye, she could see her purse. All she had to do was grab it, so she could get her knife out.

Dazzle rushed back into the room when she heard Lala scream for help. She was shocked to see Terry was trying to kill her sister. Immediately, she spotted a dumbbell weight in the corner and grabbed it.

"Get the fuck off of her." Dazzle used every ounce of energy she had left in her body to knock Terry upside the head. He doubled over in pain, but that didn't stop Dazzle from blacking out and going crazy on his ass. Viciously, she slammed the weight against his skull repeatedly. Blood squirted onto her clothes and face.

"Dazzle! Dazzle! Stop." Lala grabbed her arm. "He's dead."

The sight of his battered face and busted skull made Lala nauseous. Her stomach couldn't handle it. Hoping to her feet she rushed into the bathroom and threw up in the toilet. Dazzle finally snapped out of it and realized what she did. In a panic, she rushed inside the bathroom and grabbed some cleaning supplies. Carefully, she wiped down every place that could possibly have her fingerprints. Once everything was drowned in bleach, Lala grabbed the glasses they drank out of and tossed them into a bag, along with the semi-heavy weight. Dazzle and Lala ran into the living room and unlocked the door.

"What's that flashing red light?" Dazzle questioned.

"His alarm system. Let's go." The two opened the door and fled into the dark night.

Chapter 18

The following morning, Tori pulled up at her father's home. The same Acura was there, which meant his bastard child and the mammie was there. It was the moment she dreaded the most. Seeing him face-to-face was not what she had in mind. Especially after that bullshit stunt he pulled in Atlanta. Tori vowed never to forgive him for the mental pain he'd caused her already damaged heart.

Using her key, she walked inside and closed the door. From a distance, she could hear Diesel talking. Instead of following his voice, she went upstairs to her bedroom and closed the door. Tori had to get out of there quickly. So, she rumbled through the clothes that she brought home during the times she was in college.

Just as she tossed everything into her bag, the door swung open and there stood Diesel. "You just come into my house and not speak to me?"

Tori didn't bother to look in his direction. "We don't have anything to talk about."

"So, tell me. How is this going to work with us staying under one roof? We have to have some type of conversation, Tori. I know you're mad with me, but you have to give me a chance to explain."

"Says who?"

"I'm still your father and you live underneath my roof."

"Not anymore, I don't." Tori grabbed her bag and turned to face him. "I'll be back to get the rest of my things."

"Don't leave, Tori, please. You're my only—"

Tori cut him off immediately. "Not child."

"My only daughter. My firstborn."

"Well, now you have the son you always wanted. Be with your new family." Tori walked out the room, but then stopped in her tracks. Slowly, she turned to face him. "Now it all makes sense as to why you really wanted me out this house and in another state."

"That's not true. I did that so you can have a better future. A better life. This dope shit ain't forever. It takes away the people you love the most, if it doesn't take you out first. Someday, you'll thank me."

"You right about that. You let the dope take my mother away." Tori stormed down the hallway. That was where she encountered the unwanted houseguests.

"Hi, Tori." Torin, her little brother, looked up at her with the widest, brightly lit eyes. The anger that boiled inside of her wouldn't allow her to speak to the innocent child.

Jenna ignored the fact that she blatantly ignored her child. Right now, her only mission was to make sure that she painted a crystal-clear picture of what happened between the couple.

"Tori, can I talk to you for a moment please? I know this is really awkward and the way you found out makes it worse. I just need a chance to explain. There's more to the story you should be aware of. And I told Diesel that wasn't the way to break the news to you."

"Honestly, you don't owe me an explanation. And at this point, I couldn't care less about how any of this started. What's clear to me is you were cheating with a married man and had a baby. So, you are free to live happily ever after at this point. Whatever that is. My mom is out of the way and so am I."

Tori turned on her heels and descended down the steps and out the door. The animosity she had towards her father was bigger than one could conceive. His deception and lies over the years made her hate him. When she was a teenager, he constantly drilled her on how a man should love, cherish and respect her as a woman. That she should find someone that wouldn't cheat or put his hands on her. But lo and behold, he did the complete opposite with Bianca. *If that wasn't the pot calling the kettle black*, she thought.

After driving around aimlessly with no destination in mind, she ended up at the liquor store. In the car, she fixed a cup of Grey Goose and cranberry juice. It was about to be a long night and she didn't want to spend it alone. Rumbling through her purse, she pulled out her cellphone and called someone who could be of assistance.

"Hello, beautiful," Jude answered with a huge grin on his face.

"Hey. How are you?"

"I'm better, now that I hear your voice. How are you?"

"I'm not too good. I was just calling to see if you were busy and if I could come over. I'm in need of a few good laughs to take my mind off of the bullshit life is throwing at me." Tori hoped she wasn't being too straightforward, but at the same time, she really didn't care. She needed to be in the company of a man and Jude was that guy.

"Not at all. My door is open for you twenty-four-seven."

His comment made her blush. "I'll be there shortly."

"Okay. I'll be waiting."

It took Tori ten minutes to get to his apartment and ring the doorbell. Jude opened the door and he damn near made her faint from the chocolate deliciousness she was staring at. His chest was bulging through the white tank top he wore. His physique definitely resembled a man's that had just gotten out of prison.

"Come in." When he smiled, his gold teeth glistened.

Tori walked inside and made herself comfortable on the plush, leather sofa. Jude sat down right beside her. The goofy grin was still plastered on his handsome face.

"I'm having a hard time believing that the world is bringing trouble into my lady's life. You deserve the world at your feet."

"You have no idea." Tori raised the cup to her lips and took a sip.

"Well, that's what I'm here for. Fill me in."

Tori wasn't about to go into detail about the drama in her life, nor did she know Jude well enough to confide in him. "I rather not talk about it."

"It's that sensitive, huh?"

"It's just my dad, but I don't want to talk about it. Maybe some other time." She turned to face him with a seductive smile. "I just want you to take my mind off of it."

"I can help you with that."

"I hope so."

The alcohol had Tori feeling brave, not to mention, horny as hell. Moving closer to Jude, she straddled his lap and kissed him in the mouth. Jude couldn't resist her. Slowly, he kissed her back and slid his tongue into her mouth. Their connection was intoxicating. The kiss was erotic. It had been four years since she had sex and her body was craving the touch of a man. Tori could feel his rod stiffen against her thigh. That turned her on even more, knowing he was working with a heavy tool.

Jude's hands caressed her pillow-soft ass through her jeans. Then he made his way to the front. Anxiously, he loosened the buckle to her jeans. His hands slid inside her pants and he could feel her kitty through the black lace panties she wore. Tori started to grind in his lap, but suddenly he broke their kiss and looked into her brown eyes.

"Are you sure you want to do this?"

Her breathing was heavy. "Yes."

"Are you positive? I don't need you having any regrets in the morning."

"I'm. Sure." She pecked his lips and stood up. "You were a perfect gentleman last night, so I'm all yours right now."

Tori removed all of her clothing and tossed them to the floor. Jude's eyes widened with sexual anticipation as he examined her perky breasts, slim waist and wide hips. He couldn't help but notice the large photo of Kilo engraved in her skin. However, that wasn't going to stop him from fucking her that night.

Jude removed his threads of clothing and tossed them by her feet. Seductively, he stroked his soldier, while looking into her low, red eyes. "Come here," he demanded, while scooting to the edge of the sofa.

Tori stood in front of her chocolate savior naked as the day she was born. Slapping her thigh, he grinned. "Put your foot on the couch."

With no hesitation, she raised her leg and planted it beside him. Jude leaned in closely and licked in between her slit. Tori closed her eyes and moaned softly. Using his thumbs to part her lips, he concentrated on sucking her hardening love button. He could feel her body tremble from his touch. Jude slipped his finger inside her juicy canal and stroked her gently. One finger turned to two and two fingers turned to three. Tori's juices were pouring out, as he continued to finger her box.

Removing his fingers, he slurped them and leaned back against the sofa. "Sit on this dick."

Normally, he used a condom whenever he smashed a chick, but he didn't want to ruin the mood. Besides, he heard all about Tori and her reputation. Word on the street was shorty was stingy with the goodies and the only nigga lucky enough to smash was Kilo. Therefore, he didn't feel like he had anything to worry about.

Tori straddled his lap and gripped his piece as she slid down on it slowly. Jude filled her up completely, causing her walls to stretch and her lungs to contract. "Ahh! Shit!" She felt like a virgin all over again. It was slightly painful, but it was too late to turn back now.

Jude gripped her hips, while Tori grinded her body slowly. The tightness of her pussy wasn't what he was used to. It made him want to bust immediately, but he couldn't nut prematurely. That might kill his second chance. Thrusting his hips forward, he kept one hand on her waist, while one gripped her breast, so he could suck on her nipple.

The urge to beat her pussy down was overpowering his urge to make love to her. For the next few minutes, he allowed her to work him slowly until he gave in to his beastly desires. Raising up from the sofa, he carried her into the bedroom and laid her down on the bed. Tori was ready for what he had to offer, so she spread her legs freely and pulled him close.

"I want you to fuck me."

Jude stroked his rod just as he parted her lips and dipped inside her wet, extra tight pussy. The grip of her walls, choked his manhood. He could no longer spare her, so he pushed her legs up on his shoulders and put the pound game on her. With each thrust he delivered, their pelvises collided, making a slapping noise. Tori unknowingly squeezed her pelvic muscles and moaned loudly, hyping him up.

"Who pussy this is?" he grunted.

Tori was too busy moaning to respond.

Jude needed to hear a response, so he pushed her legs back further and rammed his dick deeper into her guts. "Answer me. Who pussy this is?"

"Yours," she screamed.

"Say it again," he demanded.

"It's yours, baby. Jude, it's yours." The pressure in her stomach would've made her say anything. He was giving her the business and it felt good. Every stroke he delivered rocked her body to the core. His fuck game was breathtaking.

"This my pussy now." He leaned down and kissed her in the mouth aggressively. "You belong to me. You my woman, so make sure every nigga know that."

"Okay! Okay!" she panted. "I'm your woman now." Tori's eyes rolled to the back of her head. "I'm cumming, baby. Shit! I'm cumming."

"That's right," he grunted. "Come for daddy, baby. Bust all over your dick."

Jude grabbed her by the waist and raised her hips. With no mercy, he beat her down until he released a heavy load into her body. With his body towering over her, he planted soft kisses on her face. "You done fucked up now. I'm not letting you go anywhere."

"Sounds like we on the same page." She smiled as she kissed him once more.

The following morning, Jude treated Tori to breakfast on the beach and a light shopping spree to show her he was serious about them being an official couple. As he pushed his Jaguar XJ through the light traffic, he clutched her hand in his.

"I hope you enjoyed your morning."

"Yes, I did. I could've did without the gifts."

Jude stole a quick glance at her. "I know, but I just want to show you that I'm serious about you."

Tori was deeply flattered and she could feel butterflies rupturing in her stomach. However, the words from her mother popped into her mind, *"Not all butterflies in your stomach equate to love. Sometimes it means that you should fear the one you're with."* Those words were loud and clear, but she pushed them out of her head.

"I hope so. It's been years since I've been in a relationship and I never thought I could move on," she confessed.

"Well, I'm here to repair your broken heart." He brought her hand up to his mouth and kissed it. "You're safe with me, Tori. I promise you that."

Chapter 19

"Girl, where the fuck you been? We been blowing up your phone all night." Lala ranted, while pacing the floor nervously, puffing on a Black & Mild.

Tori could hear the brittleness in her voice, but what she couldn't understand was the reason. The last time she checked, they were okay. "My phone went dead and you already knew I was with Jude. But what happened and why the fuck you smoking a Black?"

"We got into some real shit last night and now we scared as fuck." Lala couldn't stop pacing.

Dazzle was on the sofa biting her nails. "I can't go to prison and leave my baby out here alone."

The two of them were really blowing her, but she did her best to remain calm. "Okay...so first, I need y'all to tell me why you think you going to jail. All this panicking and talking in circles is not getting us nowhere."

"Hold on. Let me calm down." Lala took another pull from the cigar and blew the smoke out her mouth. Then she took a shot of vodka straight out the bottle. "Remember the dude Terry I was talking to?"

"Yes," Tori replied.

"He's dead," Lala blurted out like it was nothing.

"Okayyy." Tori was oblivious to what she was trying to say, but then it dawned on her. "Did you do it?"

Lala shot her glance in Dazzle's direction.

"Ah! Hell nah! What the hell happened?"

Tori sat back on the recliner and listened to Lala and Dazzle give her a complete rundown on what occurred a few hours ago. It was so much to take in that she could hardly believe they pulled such a foolish and unplanned stunt. Nonetheless, they were her girls, her sisters and she couldn't allow anything to happen to them, especially going away for life. "I need for you two to relax and I'll handle this. Write down his address."

Lala rumbled through the kitchen drawer to find a pen and paper to write on. Quickly, she scribbled down the information. Tori took the paper and shoved it into her purse. "You two stay in the house and don't come out. Try and relax and I'll take care of this."

"What are you going to do?" Dazzle's voice cracked as she questioned the next move.

"Don't worry about it. Just know it will be handled. I'll be back later." Tori walked out the door and went on a mission.

**

Detective Terrell Andrews had been with the Broward County Sheriff's Office for fifteen years. He joined the force right after high school as an officer. After five years, his savviness and wits earned him a spot as a detective. Proudly, he served the streets and helped the elderly. Some thought he was an angel here on earth, while others referred to him as Robin Hood.

The streets of Ft. Lauderdale were dark and gloomy, as usual. Light rain drops hit the windshield, as he slid down Sunrise Boulevard. Although he graduated from patrolling the streets, he just couldn't keep his ass out the hood. Detective Andrews made a quick right into Franklin Park and made his way to the well-known gambling house where the drug dealers hung out.

By the time he exited his car, the rain had stopped. Florida had the most bipolar ass weather in history. It could be cold at seven in the morning, hot by ten and raining by twelve. Terrell loved his hometown and there was no other he would rather be.

The crowd that stood underneath the carport picked up the dice and looked at the detective as he approached them casually. He could hear the mumbles and teeth sucking the closer he got.

"What's up, fellas? Who winning?"

"Why? You trying to see who you can rob tonight?" the biggest thug stated with a lot of bass and irritation in his voice.

Detective Andrews flapped his jacket backwards and placed his hand on his hip. "Hmm. I detect some hostility. I'm making the streets safe for you and your families. That's why they call me Robin Hood," he smirked.

"Nigga, please. More like robbing the hood. 'Cause you damn sho' ain't helping me and mine. You too busy taking food out my shorty's mouths and I got four of them."

"If it wasn't for me, you'd be in a six by nine in Okeechobee, nigga." Detective Andrews placed his hand on his holster and looked that Debo-looking motherfucker in the eyes. "Go and get my shit, so I can get the fuck up out of here. I got shit to do besides play around with petty ass hustlers."

The shorter thug in the group mugged him hard. "We petty hustlers, but you can't keep your broke ass from coming around here, so we can pay your pussy bill and keep the lights on for your wife. We know these crackas ain't paying you shit."

The group of thugs started laughing.

"Oh, you a funny dude. Let's see how funny shit will be when I call back-up to pick up all you bitches." Moving closer to the short thug's face, he gritted his teeth. He was so close the thug could feel his breath in his face. "And then I'll go fuck your bitch in front of your kids and make her suck my dick."

The side door squeaked and the big thug walked out with a brown paper bag clutched in his hand. He stepped in between the two men and shoved the bag into Detective Andrews' chest. "Here, man. Get up outta here."

"Nice doing business with you," he chuckled, as he walked back to his car.

There were several missed calls on his phone. When he checked the screen, he realized they were from his wife, Kelly. He called her back right away.

"You don't see me calling you?" she snapped.

"Yeah, I was handling business. What's up?"

"Your auntie keeps calling here. She been calling that son of hers and he's not answering his phone. She said it's going straight to the voicemail."

"Alright. I'm about to swing by there and holla at cuz anyway. I'll tell him to call her."

"Good, so she can stop blowing me up."

"I'll see you later on tonight."

Detective Andrews hung up the phone and slid by his cousin's house. When he arrived, there was a patrol car parked out front with the lights flickering. In a rush, he threw the car in park and jumped out. When he approached the officer, he flashed his badge.

"What's going on here?"

The officer was a tall, dorky white dude that had "rookie" lingering on his breath. He wore glasses and his face was covered with freckles. "I received a call to do a well-check."

"Did you do it?"

"Yeah."

"Is he in there?"

"Yeah, but you don't want to go in there."

"I think I do."

"We need to wait for back-up."

Detective Andrews pushed the rookie out the way and burst through the door. An eerie feeling crept over his body, as he searched frantically for his cousin. The moment he stepped into the bedroom, he completely lost it. The sight of his lifeless body brought him down to his knees. Terrell moved closer to get a better look. Terry had been bludgeoned to death. His face was disfigured beyond recognition and his head was split open to the white meat.

It was hard to keep his composure, but it was necessary. Terry sold dope, so there was no doubt in his mind that drugs were inside the house. But he couldn't let the police get ahold of that. Raising to his feet, he went inside the closet to grab the bag he often used to transport work in. To his dismay, the bag was missing. The sound of voices alerted him he was no longer alone, so he thought quickly on his feet and rushed into the guest bedroom.

Inside, Terrell opened up the closet and removed the surveillance tape and shoved it into his pocket. Then he went back into his cousin's bedroom. Kneeling down beside him, he pulled his phone out and snapped a few pictures of his dead body.

"Don't you worry, lil' bro. I'm going to catch whoever did this to you and make they asses suffer. I promise you that." Just as he stood and turned away, two officers were joining him.

"Detective." He nodded in his direction.

"Officer."

"You arrived on the scene pretty quickly. How did that happen?" he asked rhetorically.

"If you really must put that rookie mind to work, this is my cousin. Therefore, whatever information you find out, be sure to include me in it. As of right now, step aside and wait on the other detectives and crime scene to arrive." He walked off after making his point, but then he stopped abruptly and turned around. "And don't touch anything."

The rookie officer caught that insult like a pie to the face. "And where are you going?"

"I have a grieving family to comfort, if you don't mind." Detective Andrews exited the house with one thing on his mind. And that was to catch his cousin's killer. On his way out, he spotted a white Lexus that drove by slowly. The tints were too dark for him to see who was behind the wheel. His instincts said to get the tag number, but then he just brushed it off as a nosy neighbor.

The drive home was long and painful. After delivering the devastating news to his aunt, he left. The pain in her eyes wouldn't allow him to stay any longer. Anger built up inside of him as he thought about Terry's final moments of life. One thing was for certain, whoever was responsible better count their days.

Terrell walked into his four-bedroom home that he shared with his wife and two kids. Anita rushed to greet him with a hug.

"Baby, I'm so sorry for your loss. I know how much you loved Terry."

"He was like my brother."

"I know, baby."

For the first time since he discovered the body, Terrell bawled. Now that he was in the presence of his wife, he could leave that bad guy facade at the door and grieve in peace. Growing up, Terrell and Terry were raised as if they were brothers. Their mothers were sisters, so that pain ran deeper than the ocean floor.

"I'm killing everybody that had a hand in his death, I swear to God," he admitted.

Anita's heart was crushed, as she held her weeping husband. She knew he meant what he said, but she couldn't risk losing him in the process. "Baby, please allow the police to do their job and bring us justice. You can't be out here playing vigilante and you have a family. What are we supposed to do if something happens to you? Have you thought about that?"

"This is my family they took from me. I can't just sit back and not do anything," he sobbed, with snot running from his nose.

Anita felt the moisture on her shoulder, but she ignored it. "You took an oath to serve, protect, and to bring these type of people forward. God will handle whoever did this."

The gentle words she spoke were supposed to comfort him. Instead, they angered him. Terrell stood straight up with a mean scowl on his face. "When it comes to this, I'm playing God, the judge, and the jury. Justice won't be served until my hands get bloody." Terrell had his mind made up and there was nothing anyone could do to change that.

Chapter 20

Knock! Knock!

Tori stood close to the balcony, patiently waiting on the front door to open. It felt awkward showing up unannounced, but it needed to be done. Seconds later, the door became ajar and the two just stared at one another.

"Wow!" The young woman gasped like she had seen a ghost and suddenly an uneasy feeling settled on her heart.

"Hi, Tweety. How are you?"

"I'm good. How about you?" Granted, she wasn't speaking to the other girls, but she still loved Tori like a sister and was genuinely concerned.

"I'm good. I can't complain." Tori rocked on her heels and looked around before she spoke again. "So, are we going to talk right here or are you going to let me in?"

Tweety seemed a little hesitant at first, but then she laughed it off. "I'm sorry. Come in."

Both ladies sat on the brown leather sofa. Tori crossed her legs and shifted her body so they would be face-to-face. "So, what's been up with you? It's been a while and you changed your number without giving me your new one. What's up with that?"

Tweety looked away with embarrassment in her eyes. To have the one person she looked up to was heart wrenching and it made her slightly nervous. The one thing she didn't want was to be judged by one of the people that meant the world to her.

"I'm sorry," she sighed. "There were so many times I wanted to reach out to you, but I couldn't."

Tori was now puzzled. "But why?"

"I thought you were going to be on Dazzle's side." An emotional Tweety wiped her eyes that were now moist. "Tell me how trifling and nasty of a friend I was."

Tori uncrossed her leg and scooted closer to Tweety. "Don't cry. What's done is done and I'm not going to judge you. That's not my job."

Tweety opened her mouth to speak, but the little person shouting and running in the living room distracted her. "I need juice! I need juice!" He screamed, as he jumped into Tweety's arms.

"Whoa, big boy!" she laughed. "Go in the kitchen and get a Capri-Sun."

"Thank you." His voice was filled with excitement.

Tori smiled at his cuteness. "Is that your son?" The girls never mentioned that Tweety had a baby.

"No! It's Tron's baby."

"Tron? Where did he get a baby from?"

"This young girl that used to live by Dazzle."

"A young girl?" Her head jerked backwards. "How young and why do you have her baby?"

"She's a senior in high school and needed help. Her mother is on drugs, so you can imagine how that goes when you don't have a support system."

"Yeah, I can understand that." Tori nodded her head and grabbed Tweety's hand. She needed her sister to understand where she was truly coming from.

"Listen, I just want you to know I don't agree with your relationship with Tron. This is something that should've never happened, especially after the way you used to dog him out when he was with Dazzle. That makes me feel like you betrayed our sisterhood over some dick. Again, I'm not here to judge you and I do commend you for stepping in and helping this girl raise her baby. That takes a real woman to wear those shoes."

"Thanks, Tori, for being so understanding. This thing between me and Tron just happened. I never intended for this to happen. It just did."

Now the wheels in Tori's head began to turn like a windmill. "I have a question for you."

"Go ahead. Ask me anything."

"When Tron was missing on Mondays, was it you he was with?"

Tweety had a feeling that was the next question, but she was prepared to be honest once and for all. "Yes."

"Damn, Tweety, that's crazy."

"I know, but he treated me way better than he did Dazzle." Tweety peeped the stunned look on her face and attempted to clean it up. "I'm just saying his behavior was different, that's all. We all knew she nagged him and made him feel less than a man."

"That's because he wasn't a man. But to each his own. Anyway, let's change the subject."

"That'll work," she agreed.

"Well, since I'm back in town, I'm about to get shit shaking again with the dope game and this time, I'm going all the way to the top."

"I see your dream of being the Queen of the Trap hasn't died."

"Not at all. That shit is embedded in my bloodline. I'm all in until my casket drops. Which means my offer for you to join my team is still on the table. I know you have a lot on your plate, and I would like to help you lighten the load since you by yourself now."

"I appreciate the offer and I'll definitely consider it, since my finances have changed. And with Tron being locked up, it's harder on me now."

"Just let me know what you decide." Tori checked her Rolex watch. "Oh shit, I have to go. Make sure you call me. My number is the same."

"I will."

* * *

Ten minutes after Tori left her apartment, the phone rang. Tweety made a dash to pick it up. "You have a collect call from Tron. An inmate at the Okeechobee Correctional Facility. This call may be monitored or recorded. To accept charges press one, to decline charges press five." Tweety waited until the recording stopped to press one. "You may start your conversation now."

"Hey, baby," she screeched. The sound of his voice brightened her day.

"What's up, baby? How you doing?"

"I'm good. Just waiting on your call. I miss you so much."

"I miss you too. What's going on?" Tron quizzed.

"Nothing much. Just sitting here with Junior."

"Oh yeah? How my lil nigga doing?"

"He's good."

"And how is it going with his mama?"

"Things are good. Mya's doing better at taking care of him. She's working and focusing on school now. So, I'm helping out more than usual. Her mama still on drugs, so you know how that goes. She's always hounding the girl for money."

"Damn, that's crazy. I can't wait to get home."

Tweety's cheekbones were high up on her face. "Two more weeks left, baby, and I'm coming home to you."

"I can't wait."

"You ready for me to tear that pussy up?" he chuckled into the phone.

"You already know we ready for you." Tweety rocked her legs anxiously, thinking about the way Tron was going to put it down. "Oh, guess who came by the house today?"

"Who?"

"Take a guess."

"One of your homegirls must be."

"Tori."

"Oh really? What she wanted?" Tron was always fond of Tori. At one point in time, he even had a crush on her, but that all changed when he realized she only saw him as a bum ass nigga.

Tweety knew the call was being recorded. Therefore, she had to be aware of what she said and speak in codes. "She came to offer me a job at the shop."

"And what did you say?"

"I told her I will let her know."

"That's good. We gone need that when I get out." Tron smirked on the opposite end of the phone. All he needed was a plug so he could get on and get his money up. The one thing he wanted to do was help Tweety since she held him down during his whole bid. And to make sure Mya and their son was straight.

"Don't worry, baby. I got you."

"I know and that's why I love you."

"I love you too."

The fifteen-minute call was over before they knew it. Tron hung up and went back to his cell to holla at his bunkmate, Tim. He looked up at him and laughed. "You came back smiling like a muthafucka! Sis must've told you some good shit."

Tron leaned against the metal sink and chuckled. "Hell, yeah. Remember that bitch Tori I was telling you about?"

"The bitch with that money-money." Tim thought back to the conversation they had about the woman.

"Yeah. Well, apparently that bitch slid by the crib today and offered to put my girl on so she could help her." Tron rubbed his hands together. "So you know what that means?"

"A nigga about to get that duffle from that bitch."

"Fuckin' right. I'm gone use that bitch until I come out on top. Then I'm gone dismantle her whole operation, piece by fucking piece."

***

Eazy sat at his desk in deep thought, twirling a pair of stress balls in his right hand. In his left hand he clutched a glass of scotch that he casually sipped on. Ever since rumors started to recently fly about Kilo's murder, he'd been on edge. The problem was it had been so long that he didn't know what to believe and the question of *why now*, surfaced in his head. After a birdie whispered in his ear, he hit up the Chief of Police, so he could have a cold-case detective look into the accusations. Until then he had to keep a cool head and wait on a more reliable source to confirm what he felt in his heart.

The photo of Kilo and his mother that sat on his desk brought tears to his eyes. That one photo was painful to look at and it took him back to that fatal day.

It was mid-summer, Eazy and Diesel were in the yard talking to two neighborhood girls. Mr. Price pulled up into the yard and got out his Cutlass Supreme. Right away, they could tell he was drunk by the way he stumbled towards them, carrying a bottle of Seagram's Gin. No one said a word, but the teens knew how their night was going to end.

To Eazy's surprise, the house was seemingly quiet until thirty minutes passed, and he heard his mother's piercing scream. In his heart, he knew they were doing more than arguing, so he rushed into the house. When he stepped in the door, Mr. Price was choking his mother with one hand and slapping her with the other. That instantly sent him into a fit of rage.

Eazy ran up on Mr. Price and delivered several blows to the old man's head. "Get the fuck off my mama." Mr. Price fell onto the sofa, then slid to the floor. Eazy was hotter than a heater. "Hit a man, you pussy."

Mr. Price grabbed the sofa and pulled himself up to his feet, but he couldn't keep his balance. Eazy cocked back and punched him in the nose. Blood poured out instantly. The door was open, so Diesel could hear the commotion, so he ran in to see what was going on. He was surprised at the sight.

"Aye, what's going on?" He took one look at his father and shook his head. As bad as he wanted to defend his father, he couldn't. Mr. Price was wrong and he knew it.

"He needs to get out, that's what's wrong." Pamela screamed.

Diesel tried to help his father, but he declined. "I don't need help. I'm leaving."

Later on that night, Eazy couldn't sleep, so he rode around with one of his young chicks blowing smoke and drinking. The young chick was tipsy and started talking too much. "You know your daddy cheating on your mama with a lady named Pearl. I always see him at her house."

"What?" Eazy frowned.

"Yeah. He be over there by my house. I be seeing his Cutlass. She said that's her boyfriend."

"Oh yeah?"

"Yep."

Eazy gripped the steering wheel tight. Every thought he had in his head about smashing the chick went out the window for the moment. He was now focused on revenge instead. Pulling up to the intersection, he busted a U-turn and pulled into the motel. Pulling out the key, he passed it to her. "Go in the room. I'll be right back."

"Why? I'm horny."

"I need to bust this lick first. Go shower and I'll be right back."

"Hurry up too." She snatched the key from his hand and got out the car. Eazy watched her closely until she made it inside. Then he pulled off. Fifteen minutes later, he was pulling up into the young chick's neighborhood and drove down her street.

Anger boiled inside of him the second he spotted Mr. Price's car parked alongside the road. Eazy turned off his lights and parked behind the car. Cautiously, he looked around at the houses to make sure no one could see him. There were no lights on in anyone's home, so he got out the car with a pair of wire cutters in his hand. Getting down on the ground, he slid under the car and cut the brake lines. "I got something for your bitch ass." When he was finished, he ran back to his car and peeled off.

Eazy opened his eyes and shook the buried secret from his head. Just the thought of all the bad shit he did in his life made him feel like the death of his son was bad karma. That alone made him want to do right. With that being said, he picked up his phone and dialed a number that hadn't used in years. The phone rang a long time before someone answered.

"Hello."

"We need to talk." Eazy sat his glass down on the table.

"Who is this calling my house phone?"

"Eazy."

Diesel was surprised because his was the last voice he thought he would hear. "Talk about what?"

"I've been doing a lot of thinking and it's time we sit down and call a truce. We were once close and I want us to change that. Me and you were like brothers. And with Tori living with me, I don't want no beef in the air."

Diesel wanted to hang up, but it was his fault they were divided in the first place. Instead of sticking to his guns, he decided to take the high road. "You're right. We can do that."

"How does tomorrow sound?"

"That'll work."

"A'ight. I'll hit you with the details."

"Hold up. You said Tori is living with you?"

"Yeah."

Diesel couldn't believe what he was hearing. "I didn't know that."

"Yeah, she was having a hard time living in the house Kilo bought her. So, she's staying here until she sells it. At the end of the day, she's still my daughter-in-law."

Diesel was ready to hang up. "Hit me tomorrow. I'll be ready."

Eazy hung up the phone feeling as if a heavy burden had been lifted from his shoulders. If karma was coming back to haunt him, he needed to make things right for Honcho's sake. Just then his phone rang and when he looked at the screen, it was the Chief calling.

"I have some good news for you, my brother." An evil smile spread across his lips, as he listened to the information that floated into his ear. When the Chief was done explaining everything to him, he called for back-up.

Chapter 21

Tori's eyes flung open from a not-so pleasant sleep. The majority of her night was spent with her tossing and turning. The memory of her dream disappeared without a trace. Her heart's rhythm ran a marathon inside her chest cavity and her breathing was harsh. Using her left hand, she patted her chest to calm herself down.

"Whew! Calm down, Tori. It was just a dream."

Tori rolled over on her side in the king sized bed and stared at the clock. It was a quarter after five and the room was dark. The sun wasn't due to set on the horizon for another hour and some change.

"It's definitely not time to get up."

Tori then closed her eyes and attempted to fall asleep. But in her head, she could hear the constant whisper of Bianca's voice, telling her to get up. Ignoring it, she placed the pillow over her head and covered it with a blanket. Bianca continued to whisper, *get up*, in her baby girl's ear. It wasn't the first time she'd heard her voice.

A frustrated Tori threw the covers back, while grunting. "Mommy, what's wrong? What are you trying to tell me?"

Once those questions left her lips, it dawned on her. It was Bianca's birthday. The minute she acknowledged the spirit with a *Happy Birthday*, she was able to get some sleep.

Five hours later, Tori found herself at the cemetery, sitting on the grass and clutching her mother's diary. "Happy Birthday, Mommy. I brought your favorite flowers."

The neatly trimmed grass was essential to the beautiful sunflowers she picked up along the way. Tori pulled a bottle of rum from her purse and twisted off the cap. Placing the bottle against her lips, she took a shot, then poured a shot into the grass. "Drink up, baby."

Sweet memories played in her mind, as the cool breeze made her hair sway in the wind. The images were vivid like a movie being played on a projector screen. Bianca may have had an addiction, but she still had Tori's best intentions at heart. She wanted Tori to have a better life and get out from under Diesel's tight grip. No matter how much powder she'd snorted or shot into her veins, Bianca was still her number-one girl. Tori thumbed through the diary and stopped on the first entry her finger landed on.

February 3, 2008

This fucking therapist is making me write in this stupid ass diary about my feelings and shit and I don't like it. I'm a grown ass, emotionless ass woman who thinks this shit is childish. My feelings died years ago, thanks to Diesel. I would rather gouge my eyes out with a pencil than be doing this bullshit. Actually, I would rather be higher than Cooter Brown. But nooo, I'm being forced to dig up old rubbish and buried secrets.

Diesel keeps asking me what's wrong, as if he didn't know. He must've thought I was so stupid. That I was oblivious to what was happening around me. He was cheating. And with a young slut bucket at that.

According to my reliable source, it had been going on for a long time. Did it hurt when I found out? No. I hadn't loved Diesel in years. Not since I was shot and lost my son. THAT'S WHAT HURTS ME!! That was when the HATE began. It was all his fault too. All he had to do was keep his dick in his pants and that incident would've never occurred.

But no, he had to sleep with his brother's wife. So, in return, I fucked his brother. We knew it was wrong, but we were hurting. We found comfort in each other's arms. We were angry. We wanted revenge. And the best REVENGE was best served COLD!

*** *

The click-clack sounds of arsenal weapons being locked and loaded was the only noise that could be heard coming from the kitchen. Eazy laid his MAC-10 on the table and folded his hands.

"As you all know, catching Kilo's killers has been a long time coming. I need everybody ready to light some shit up. If you having second thoughts, you know where to find the door."

The group of men all agreed they were ready.

"Good, because I have been anticipating this moment for years and my prayers have finally been answered. It's time to take this muthafucka out."

Honcho walked into the kitchen and froze when he saw the gang picking up their weapons. An eerie feeling settled in his stomach, out of fear about what his father was about to engage in. "Pops, what's going on. What are you doing?"

"About to end the life of the muthafucka that killed your brother." He gritted his teeth, as he walked towards his youngest son.

"I don't think that's a good idea."

Eazy patted him on the shoulder. "That's why I didn't ask you. Stay in the house. It's much safer for you." Eazy pushed on with his foot soldiers trailing behind him.

Honcho waited until the door closed before he pulled out his cellphone to send a warning.

***

The phone call Tori received cut her visit at the cemetery short. The sound of her screeching tires frightened the other families were visiting their loved ones. Flushing it down State Road Seven, up to Atlantic Boulevard, Tori hopped onto the turnpike and did one hundred miles an hour to Deerfield Beach. With the high rate of speed she traveled, Tori was able to cut the trip by half the time.

Just as she cut her speed to make the exit, the blaring sound of police sirens brought it all to an end. Tori pushed through the toll and pulled over on the shoulder. Immediately, she reached into her purse to retrieve her driver's license and registration out of the glovebox. The officer approached her vehicle and tapped on the window.

"License and registration please."

Tori passed the documents through the window and kept her eyes forward. The last thing she needed was a confrontation with a trigger-happy cop. He was already interfering with her mission, so there was no need to make the situation worse than what it really was.

"Do you know why I stopped you?"

Her eyes remained forward. "Speeding."

"Yeah. You were doing one hundred miles an hour in a sixty-five-mile zone."

"I know. Can you just write my ticket so I can leave, please? I'm in a rush right now. Thanks."

The officer was hoping her license was suspended or she had an active warrant, so he could arrest her. The attitude she displayed was pushing every button on his red neck.

"Be right back."

Nervously, Tori sat in the car rocking her legs. For every minute that passed she grew more and more agitated. All she wanted was her ticket so she could get the fuck on. As far as she knew, the situation could be unfolding as she spoke. That was when she decided to call Diesel. The phone rang constantly before it went to voicemail.

***

Diesel sat his phone down on the counter, as he watched Tori call him repeatedly. True indeed, he wanted to speak to his daughter, but her timing was bad. He was on a mission and couldn't afford to be distracted. On his way out the door, he was stopped by Jenna, when she grabbed a hold of his arm.

"Papi, no quiero que vayas a pelear una batalla que no es tuya," Jenna babbled.

"English, baby," he replied calmly.

"Papi, I don't want you going out there to fight a battle that isn't yours. What if you get hurt, arrested or even worse, killed? What will me and the baby do without you?" Diesel knew she was concerned. He could see the tears welling up in her eyes.

Gently, he placed his hand on her neck and kissed her lips. "Hey, everything is going to be okay. It will take Jesus and his disciples to take me down and they ain't nowhere around. An old friend of mine needs my help and I promised to do that. My word is all I have."

"But we're your family and we need you."

"I know that baby, but he needs me too. I promise that I'll be back." Diesel wasn't one hundred percent sure that everything will go as planned, but he couldn't risk telling her that. "I'm leaving my phone here, so you won't be able to call me. You'll be able to see me when I get back, okay?"

Jenna didn't want to agree, but what other choice did she have. Once his mind was made up, there was no changing it. "I love you, baby. Please come back home in one piece."

"I will, I promise." Diesel walked out the door and hopped into the black Chevy Suburban.

***

Eazy sat inside the warehouse, waiting anxiously for his guests to arrive. His mind were on Kilo and his last moments of life. Every time he thought about the way his son suffered, it angered him. And the fact that it took so long for him to find the person who was responsible for his early demise, infuriated him. Eazy had high hopes on watching his son go down the aisle and have kids. That was the one thing he embedded in his boys, find a good woman, settle down, have kids and take care of their families. It hurt his heart that Kilo could never fulfill his wishes.

"You good, my G?" Fabian, his right-hand man and Kilo's god daddy could notice the glassiness in his eyes. Just like Eazy, he took a major loss when his godson was killed. For the twenty-one years Kilo was on earth, he was in his life since the day he was born. So, in his eyes, he had lost his son as well.

"Honestly, brother, I'll never be good. You know me and Kilo had a unique bond. He was my heart and soul."

Fabian placed his hand on his shoulder. "I know, brother, but we still have Honcho out here."

"It's different with Honcho. I love him too, but that's the good son. Kilo was my twin, my replica and this pussy ass nigga took my boy out this world like he was his creator." Eazy nodded his head. "But I'm gone make sure this nigga join him. This nigga about to take a permanent dirt nap with the maggots."

One of the young shooters ran inside with his strap clutched tightly in his hand. "Aye boss, these niggas coming up the block."

Eazy jumped up, grabbed his MAC-10 and ran to the exit. The sight of the black Suburban cruising up the street filled Eazy's heart with anticipation. His pointer finger itched, as he placed it on the trigger. As soon as the truck pulled up in front of them, Eazy squeezed the trigger and let it rip from the .38 extended clip.

Fraaaack! Fraaaack!

As instructed, his boys waited until he got off first before they jumped in and flooded the truck with bullet holes. *Boc! Boc! Boc!*

Fraaaack! Fraaaack!

The gunfire lasted for approximately two minutes. By the time the smoke, cleared the truck was riddled with bullets. The occupants of the vehicle never had a chance to get a single round off. Eazy was finally able to smile as they took off running and peeling out into the afternoon sun.

***

Tori finally pulled up to Eazy's house after being stopped by the redneck cop. Honcho was standing outside waiting on her. Expeditiously, he hopped into the car and she pulled off. "Where are they going?" she asked frantically.

"To the warehouses on SW 10th Street," he admitted.

"How do you know he's going to kill my dad? And what makes him think Diesel was behind Kilo's death?"

Honcho shrugged his shoulders. "Honestly, sis, I don't know. He wouldn't tell me. All I know is word finally came back that it was Diesel who put the hit out on Kilo." Honcho sat in the passenger seat and reflected on his memories with his only brother.

"I can't believe this shit."

"Why not? You knew Diesel didn't want you and Kilo together. It all makes sense." Honcho turned to look at Tori. "Don't you think so?"

Tori thought long and hard about her feelings towards Diesel. True enough, she hated his ways and him but at the same time, the fact still remained that he was her father. But Kilo was technically her husband. "Baby bro, all I can say is, I wouldn't put shit past Diesel. He has surprised me in more ways than one. But I would hate to think he would intentionally hurt me beyond repair by killing the love of my life."

Honcho and Tori remained silent until they hit SW 10th Street and turned off on the back street. When she hit the curb, Tori immediately spotted several police cars on the scene. Mashing down on the gas, Tori sped up, doing sixty miles an hour until she was directly behind a police car. Slamming on brakes, she hopped out the car with Honcho on her trail and ran up to the crime scene. The sight of her father's truck made her have a fit. Tori was screaming and hollering as she tried to approach the truck, but the police grabbed her.

"Let me go. That's my daddy," she cried. Honcho grabbed her from behind and tried to restrain her. "Daddy! Daddy! Nooo!" she screamed and fought, trying to get loose.

To Be Continued...
Dope Girl 2: Pretty Girls Run the Trap
Coming Soon

Submission Guideline

Submit the first three chapters of your completed manuscript to ldpsubmissions@gmail.com, subject line: Your book's title. The manuscript must be in a .doc file and sent as an attachment. Document should be in Times New Roman, double spaced and in size 12 font. Also, provide your synopsis and full contact information. If sending multiple submissions, they must each be in a separate email.

Have a story but no way to send it electronically? You can still submit to LDP/Ca$h Presents. Send in the first three chapters, written or typed, of your completed manuscript to:

LDP: Submissions Dept
Po Box 870494
Mesquite, Tx 75187

DO NOT send original manuscript. Must be a duplicate.

Provide your synopsis and a cover letter containing your full contact information.

Thanks for considering LDP and Ca$h Presents.

Coming Soon from Lock Down Publications/Ca$h Presents

BOW DOWN TO MY GANGSTA

By **Ca$h**

TORN BETWEEN TWO

By **Coffee**

THE STREETS STAINED MY SOUL **II**

By **Marcellus Allen**

BLOOD OF A BOSS **VI**

SHADOWS OF THE GAME II

By **Askari**

LOYAL TO THE GAME **IV**

By **T.J. & Jelissa**

A DOPEBOY'S PRAYER **II**

By **Eddie "Wolf" Lee**

IF LOVING YOU IS WRONG… **III**

By **Jelissa**

TRUE SAVAGE **VII**

MIDNIGHT CARTEL III

DOPE BOY MAGIC III

By **Chris Green**

BLAST FOR ME **III**

A SAVAGE DOPEBOY III

CUTTHROAT MAFIA II

By **Ghost**

A HUSTLER'S DECEIT III

KILL ZONE **II**

BAE BELONGS TO ME III

By **Aryanna**

THE COST OF LOYALTY **III**

By **Kweli**

CHAINED TO THE STREETS II

By **J-Blunt**

KING OF NEW YORK V

COKE KINGS IV

BORN HEARTLESS IV

By **T.J. Edwards**

GORILLAZ IN THE BAY V

TEARS OF A GANGSTA II

De'Kari

THE STREETS ARE CALLING II

Duquie Wilson

KINGPIN KILLAZ IV

STREET KINGS III

PAID IN BLOOD III

CARTEL KILLAZ IV

Hood Rich

SINS OF A HUSTLA II

ASAD

TRIGGADALE III

Elijah R. Freeman

KINGZ OF THE GAME V

Playa Ray

SLAUGHTER GANG IV

RUTHLESS HEART III

By Willie Slaughter

THE HEART OF A SAVAGE III

By Jibril Williams

FUK SHYT II

By Blakk Diamond

THE DOPEMAN'S BODYGAURD II

By Tranay Adams

TRAP GOD II

By Troublesome

YAYO III

A SHOOTER'S AMBITION II

By S. Allen

GHOST MOB

Stilloan Robinson

KINGPIN DREAMS II

By Paper Boi Rari

CREAM

By Yolanda Moore

SON OF A DOPE FIEND II

By Renta

FOREVER GANGSTA II

By Adrian Dulan

LOYALTY AIN'T PROMISED II

By Keith Williams

THE PRICE YOU PAY FOR LOVE II

DOPE GIRL MAGIC II

By Destiny Skai

THE LIFE OF A HOOD STAR

By Rashia Wilson

TOE TAGZ III

By Ah'Million

CONFESSIONS OF A GANGSTA II

By Nicholas Lock

PAID IN KARMA III

By **Meesha**

I'M NOTHING WITHOUT HIS LOVE II

By Monet Dragun

CAUGHT UP IN THE LIFE II

By Robert Baptiste

NEW TO THE GAME II

Dope Girl Magic

By **Malik D. Rice**

Life of a Savage II

By **Romell Tukes**

Quiet Money II

By **Trai'Quan**

Available Now

RESTRAINING ORDER **I & II**

By **CA$H & Coffee**

LOVE KNOWS NO BOUNDARIES **I II & III**

By **Coffee**

RAISED AS A GOON I, II, III & IV

BRED BY THE SLUMS I, II, III

BLAST FOR ME I & II

ROTTEN TO THE CORE I II III

A BRONX TALE I, II, III

DUFFEL BAG CARTEL I II III IV

HEARTLESS GOON I II III IV

A SAVAGE DOPEBOY I II

HEARTLESS GOON I II III

DRUG LORDS I II III

CUTTHROAT MAFIA

By **Ghost**

LAY IT DOWN **I & II**

LAST OF A DYING BREED

BLOOD STAINS OF A SHOTTA I & II III

By **Jamaica**

LOYAL TO THE GAME I II III

LIFE OF SIN I, II III

By **TJ & Jelissa**

BLOODY COMMAS I & II

SKI MASK CARTEL I II & III

KING OF NEW YORK I II,III IV

RISE TO POWER I II III

COKE KINGS I II III

BORN HEARTLESS I II III

By **T.J. Edwards**

IF LOVING HIM IS WRONG…I & II

LOVE ME EVEN WHEN IT HURTS I II III

By **Jelissa**

WHEN THE STREETS CLAP BACK I & II III

THE HEART OF A SAVAGE I II

By **Jibril Williams**

A DISTINGUISHED THUG STOLE MY HEART I II & III

LOVE SHOULDN'T HURT I II III IV

RENEGADE BOYS I II III IV

PAID IN KARMA I II

By **Meesha**

A GANGSTER'S CODE I &, II III

A GANGSTER'S SYN I II III

THE SAVAGE LIFE I II III

CHAINED TO THE STREETS

By J-Blunt

PUSH IT TO THE LIMIT

By **Bre' Hayes**

BLOOD OF A BOSS **I, II, III, IV, V**

SHADOWS OF THE GAME

By **Askari**

THE STREETS BLEED MURDER **I, II & III**

THE HEART OF A GANGSTA I II& III

By **Jerry Jackson**

CUM FOR ME I II III IV V

An **LDP Erotica Collaboration**

BRIDE OF A HUSTLA **I II & II**

THE FETTI GIRLS **I, II& III**

CORRUPTED BY A GANGSTA I, II III, IV

BLINDED BY HIS LOVE

THE PRICE YOU PAY FOR LOVE

DOPE GIRL MAGIC

By **Destiny Skai**

WHEN A GOOD GIRL GOES BAD

By **Adrienne**

THE COST OF LOYALTY I II

By Kweli

A GANGSTER'S REVENGE **I II III & IV**

THE BOSS MAN'S DAUGHTERS I II III IV V

A SAVAGE LOVE **I & II**

BAE BELONGS TO ME I II

A HUSTLER'S DECEIT I, II, III

WHAT BAD BITCHES DO I, II, III

SOUL OF A MONSTER I II III

KILL ZONE

By **Aryanna**

A KINGPIN'S AMBITON

A KINGPIN'S AMBITION **II**

I MURDER FOR THE DOUGH

By **Ambitious**

TRUE SAVAGE I II III IV V VI

DOPE BOY MAGIC I, II

MIDNIGHT CARTEL I II

By **Chris Green**

A DOPEBOY'S PRAYER

By **Eddie "Wolf" Lee**

THE KING CARTEL **I, II & III**

Dope Girl Magic

By **Frank Gresham**

THESE NIGGAS AIN'T LOYAL **I, II & III**

By **Nikki Tee**

GANGSTA SHYT **I II &III**

By **CATO**

THE ULTIMATE BETRAYAL

By **Phoenix**

BOSS'N UP **I , II & III**

By **Royal Nicole**

I LOVE YOU TO DEATH

By Destiny J

I RIDE FOR MY HITTA

I STILL RIDE FOR MY HITTA

By **Misty Holt**

LOVE & CHASIN' PAPER

By **Qay Crockett**

TO DIE IN VAIN

SINS OF A HUSTLA

By **ASAD**

BROOKLYN HUSTLAZ

By **Boogsy Morina**

BROOKLYN ON LOCK I & II

By **Sonovia**

GANGSTA CITY

By **Teddy Duke**
A DRUG KING AND HIS DIAMOND I & II III
A DOPEMAN'S RICHES
HER MAN, MINE'S TOO I, II
CASH MONEY HO'S
By Nicole Goosby
TRAPHOUSE KING **I II & III**
KINGPIN KILLAZ I II III
STREET KINGS I II
PAID IN BLOOD **I II**
CARTEL KILLAZ I II III
By **Hood Rich**
LIPSTICK KILLAH **I, II, III**
CRIME OF PASSION I II & III
By **Mimi**
STEADY MOBBN' **I, II, III**
THE STREETS STAINED MY SOUL
By **Marcellus Allen**
WHO SHOT YA **I, II, III**
SON OF A DOPE FIEND
Renta
GORILLAZ IN THE BAY **I II III IV**
TEARS OF A GANGSTA
DE'KARI

TRIGGADALE I II

Elijah R. Freeman

GOD BLESS THE TRAPPERS I, II, III

THESE SCANDALOUS STREETS I, II, III

FEAR MY GANGSTA I, II, III

THESE STREETS DON'T LOVE NOBODY I, II

BURY ME A G I, II, III, IV, V

A GANGSTA'S EMPIRE I, II, III, IV

THE DOPEMAN'S BODYGAURD

Tranay Adams

THE STREETS ARE CALLING

Duquie Wilson

MARRIED TO A BOSS... I II III

By Destiny Skai & Chris Green

KINGZ OF THE GAME I II III IV

Playa Ray

SLAUGHTER GANG I II III

RUTHLESS HEART I II

By Willie Slaughter

FUK SHYT

By Blakk Diamond

DON'T F#CK WITH MY HEART I II

By Linnea

ADDICTED TO THE DRAMA I II III

By Jamila

YAYO I II

A SHOOTER'S AMBITION

By S. Allen

TRAP GOD

By Troublesome

FOREVER GANGSTA

By Adrian Dulan

TOE TAGZ I II

By Ah'Million

KINGPIN DREAMS

By Paper Boi Rari

CONFESSIONS OF A GANGSTA

By Nicholas Lock

I'M NOTHING WITHOUT HIS LOVE

By Monet Dragun

CAUGHT UP IN THE LIFE

By Robert Baptiste

NEW TO THE GAME

By **Malik D. Rice**

Life of a Savage

By **Romell Tukes**

LOYALTY AIN'T PROMISED

By Keith Williams

Quiet Money

By **Trai'Quan**

BOOKS BY LDP'S CEO, CA$H

TRUST IN NO MAN

TRUST IN NO MAN 2

TRUST IN NO MAN 3

BONDED BY BLOOD

SHORTY GOT A THUG

THUGS CRY

THUGS CRY 2

THUGS CRY 3

TRUST NO BITCH

TRUST NO BITCH 2

TRUST NO BITCH 3

TIL MY CASKET DROPS

RESTRAINING ORDER

RESTRAINING ORDER 2

IN LOVE WITH A CONVICT

Coming Soon

BONDED BY BLOOD 2

BOW DOWN TO MY GANGSTA

Dope Girl Magic

CPSIA information can be obtained
at www.ICGtesting.com
Printed in the USA
LVHW011509020620
657245LV00012B/1069